I FOUND TREASURE IN WANNABE MICHIGAN

Roy M. Bambach

ISBN 0-7414-3840-2

Published by:

INFINITY
PUBLISHING.COM

1094 New DeHaven Street, Suite 100
West Conshohocken, PA 19428-2713
Info@buybooksontheweb.com
www.buybooksontheweb.com
Toll-free (877) BUY BOOK
Local Phone (610) 941-9999
Fax (610) 941-9959

Printed in the United States of America

Printed on Recycled Paper

Published April 2007

Dedication

To my late wife Brenda Mae Bambach:

Thank you sweetheart for your ability to inspire me to do great things…For this I will always love you.

Acknowledgments

I would like to express my gratitude to certain individuals whose assistance made this book possible.

To Brenda Falk, who spent many hours proofreading as well as giving assistance with the content.

To Shannon (Bambach) Underwood, who encouraged me to be persistent in my writing and to follow my dreams.

To the rest of my children, Thomas and Samantha Bambach, who are supportive with their dad's writing career.

And to countless others who are too numerous to list.

Contents

CHAPTER 1

UNCERTAIN FUTURE

"Hey, there it is!" my mother squealed excitedly, as she repeatedly jabbed her elbow into my ribs. "Wake up, Junior, we're here!" She reached over, grabbed me and began shaking me as if I were a rag doll.

"All right, all right!" I said, trying to get her to stop. "I'm awake!"

My father lifted his foot off the gas pedal and pushed in the clutch. The old rattle trap, the name I so affectionately gave to my father's truck, shuddered to a stop.

He pointed towards some faded words painted on a weathered sign hanging at the side of the road. "Welcome to Wannabe!" he announced. "That's what the sign says."

"That's right!" my mother agreed, trying to contain her excitement. "And this is where we're going to spend the rest of our lives!" As my father slowly drove into town, open farm fields gave way to old brick homes with neatly kept lawns. Tall, majestic elm trees lined each side of the road; they reminded me of tall telephone poles back in the city.

The big city… that was the place where I grew up. I was perfectly happy living in a big city. Why wouldn't I be? It was the 1950's and things were finally happening for me! I was a freshman in high school and eagerly looking forward to getting my driver's license. Even girls were beginning to notice me. Everything finally seemed to be going my way…or so it seemed. Then one day out of nowhere, like a bomb shell, my parents informed me my father no longer had a job, and we would have no choice but to sell our house and move. They said that fortunately for us, one of my father's old army buddies, a Mr. Jonathon Zinker, offered him, how did my mother put it, "An opportunity of a lifetime." My father could have a job at Mr. Zinker's lumberyard, and as part of the deal, he'd throw in an old fixer-upper house at a great price. What did I get out of this so-called deal? A chance to move into a crummy, old house in a one-horse nowhere town named Wannabe!

"Wannabe is a nice little town," my mother said, as we slowed down to make a right turn. We pulled off the road and into a corner gas station. Did I just say gas station? Well, at least that's what it said on the sign. To me it looked more like a combination used toilet and army surplus store. Toilets of all shapes, colors and sizes were neatly stacked in rows along one side of the old block building, while on the opposite side, old army jeeps and assorted car parts lay heaped in rusting scrap piles.

"We need gas," my father announced, as we rolled to a stop next to the gas pump. He turned the engine off and got out; my mother climbed over me and followed after him.

"Want a cold soda, Junior?" my mother called out, as she grabbed onto my father's arm.

Before I could even answer, an old man, who looked as if he hadn't shaven or bathed in a month leaned in through the open window of the truck and just about scared me to death. He was dressed in overalls, and his face looked all dried and wrinkly, as if he had spent one too many years baking in the hot sun. "Hello, young fellow, my name is Wilson," he announced, as he surveyed the inside of the truck. He put out his hand and smiled. I forced a smile on my face and reluctantly shook his hand.

"My name is Junior, Junior Wolfe," I answered.

"Where you folks heading?" he asked. He smiled again, and I noticed he had several missing teeth.

"Wannabe," I replied, not that I thought it was any of his business.

"Well now, Junior, looks like you've come to the right place," he said.

A second man, who seemed to know this Wilson fellow, came over and joined him.

"Looks like somebody's moving," the other man commented, as he snooped around the back of the truck.

"The boy and his parents bought a house here in Wannabe," Wilson replied. "It's probably the old Zinker farm."

"Nobody in his right mind would buy that place!" the other man said, shaking his head. "I'll bet it's the Moore farm!"

Then without saying another word to me, the two men turned and slowly walked back towards the gas station arguing back and forth about which one was right. It was as if they were in their own little world. I shook my head.

"Strange!" I said out loud.

My mother returned and handed me my soda through the truck window. "Whom were you talking to?" she asked.

"Just some old geezers," I replied, as I touched the cold bottle of soda to my forehead.

She stared at me for a moment. "I don't think that was very nice!" she scolded. "They looked quite harmless to me."

Rather than apologize, I just shrugged my shoulders and looked away.

A short, overweight man, dressed in overalls and no shirt, came out from inside the gas station and followed my father back to the truck.

"What next?" I said to myself. The fat man nodded and said hello as he began pumping our gas. As I stared, I couldn't help but notice he was completely bald; and the sweat on his head reflected the bright sun like a mirror.

"That guy could stand to lose some weight," I whispered, half jokingly. The fat man pulled a hanky from his back pocket and dabbed sweat off his face.

"That's Arthur Stubbs," my father responded, as he got back into the truck. "We were told he used to deliver newspapers, and now he wants to compete in the Olympics." My father waved at the man when he finished filling the gas tank.

"That guy in the Olympics?" I asked. "You've got to be kidding!" My father acted as if he hadn't heard me and started the truck. We pulled out and headed north on Union

Street. Just a stone's throw from the gas station, two sets of train tracks crossed Union Street running east and west. My father slowed down and stopped at the edge of the tracks.

"Did I tell you that our new house is near these railroad tracks, Junior?" my mother asked, poking her elbow into my ribs again. Somehow I got the distinct impression she was trying to convince me it was going to be exciting living next to a bunch of loud trains. My father pulled forward and drove over the tracks and then slowed down a second time.

"There it is, Junior!" my mother said, pointing. "That's the house!" Up ahead, sitting right on the corner of Pine and Union Streets was an old, two-story farmhouse partially obscured by several half-dead willow trees. I closed my eyes as we turned the corner and came to a stop.

"This is a dream. This is a dream," I whispered over and over. When I opened my eyes, we were…you guessed it, sitting right in front of that old house. I stared in disbelief at the run-down place; it was worse than I'd imagined. The place looked as if it hadn't been lived in since the Civil War. Most of the white paint on the house had curled and fallen off, exposing the bare wood. From what I could see, most of the glass in the windows was either cracked or missing. At the end of the driveway stood a huge barn that towered over the house, looking to be in no better condition than the house. I turned and looked at my parents, *what in the world were they thinking*? At that very moment, I was feeling anger and contempt for what they'd done, or should I say, were about to do. They, on the other hand, had this look of bliss on their faces, as if they had convinced themselves this was going to be the greatest adventure in the world! I just shook my head, thinking they were both crazy.

I've always had this picture in my mind of the perfect farmhouse out in the country. You know… the ones you see on calendars. They're always set far off the road at the top of a tree-covered hill. This old farmhouse was so close to the road, you could spit out the living room window and hit a car that was going by. Well, so much for the perfect farmhouse. My father pulled forward then backed up into the driveway.

"Smell that fresh air?" my father asked, as he got out of the truck. He pounded his chest as if he were some kind of gorilla. I got out and took a deep breath.

"If I didn't know better, I'd swear the air smelled like pigs to me," I remarked, sarcastically.

My parents began to eagerly untie the massive load in the back of the truck while I just stood there watching.

"Junior, why don't you take the twenty-five cent tour of the place while your mother and I get some of this stuff off the truck?" my father suggested.

At this point, I wasn't sure I wanted to take the twenty-five cent tour. This place wasn't worth twenty-five cents! I turned and walked towards the house, noticing several 'no trespassing' signs nailed to the weathered siding. A 'house condemned' sign hung on the front door, and it gently swung back and forth in the breeze.

"Couldn't they just have bought a circus tent or an old school bus?" I said out loud. "Anything would be better than this." I headed around back of the house only to find the backyard a mass of overgrown weeds, willow bushes, and nasty prickers. It was like walking in a mine field in no-man's land! I took a few steps and a rabbit darted out in front of me. I watched it as it ran toward a miniature sized house in the back yard. I stared at the strange little house for a moment and wondered why anyone would build such a thing. The odd little structure was painted white with two doors hanging side by side; I thought it strange having two doors. Above the two doors, a small sign was hung with the faded words, "Welcome to the Two-Hole Inn." I walked towards the little building, all the while looking around to see if anybody was watching. Seeing my parents were busily going in and out of the house like bees around a beehive, I carefully reached for one of the door handles and pulled it open. In an instant, it was very clear what I'd just discovered.

"It's an outhouse, a two person outhouse!" I mumbled amazedly. When I slammed the door closed, the little building shook and instantly, hundreds of huge yellow and black bees came swarming out from the inside. Not wanting to find out what it's like to be attacked by a thousand angry bees, I turned and ran back to the house, narrowly making my escape by slipping behind a screened entrance door on the driveway side of the house.

After the sound of the buzzing bees faded and I was sure I was safe, I turned around and realized I was in the kitchen. The place looked like something out of a museum. It had an old stove, an antique refrigerator, and an old wooden table with four chairs. The phone that hung on the wall looked so old it could have belonged to Thomas Edison. From the kitchen, I walked through a doorway that lead into the living room which, like the kitchen, was also full of old furniture. As I studied a portrait on the wall of an older couple, I could hear the faint blast of a train whistle off in the distance. I turned and walked across the room and stood at the windows that faced the front yard. A warm breeze blew into the living room through the broken windows, and I wondered for a moment if the bees knew how easy it would be to get into this house…I shuddered at the thought.

As I stared out the windows, the crossing lights began to flash; and I knew the train would be here soon. Suddenly, as if the house had fallen off its foundation, it began to shake making the floor feel as if it was swaying back and forth. The wooden sashes in the old windows began to slide up and down making odd creaking noises, and the ceiling light began swaying back and forth. I watched in horror as bits of loose plaster tumbled off the walls and fell to the floor. Furniture that looked as if it hadn't been moved in years suddenly began sliding around the room as if they had wheels. Now convinced that the train was going to shake the house into pieces, with me in it, I ran back through the kitchen and outside as fast as I could. I found my parents out in the driveway staring at the train like two excited children, totally oblivious to what was happening to their precious house. It was as if they didn't want to move an inch until the very last car had disappeared from sight.

Finally, after the excitement was over, my father turned and put his hand on my shoulder, as if he was going to say something profound. "Isn't it great being able to see the trains this close?" he asked.

I rolled my eyes. "Sure, Pop, it's great," I said, as I brushed plaster dust off my clothes. "This is just great."

Even after my parents had gone back up to the house, I continued to stare at the train tracks. *How in the world am I going to get through all of this? I've been here for a matter of minutes and already I've been attacked by bees and almost crushed to death by a train. What more could possibly happen to me?* I wondered.

"Junior!" my mother called out. "Your father needs your help around in back of the house." I turned to see her hanging out the kitchen window.

"What in the world is he doing?" I asked, as I walked past my mother. She just smiled.

"You'll see," she replied.

From an open basement window, I could hear my father calling out; and I knelt down and peeked inside. I guess I shouldn't have been surprised, considering what I've seen so far. My father was dressed in a pair of old fishing waders splashing around in knee-deep water in the basement.

"Take this hose, Junior, and pull it through the window," he instructed, as he handed me one end. "I'm going to hook this end to a water pump."

"Hey, Pop, you sure you wouldn't rather keep this water down here?" I asked. "We could have our own fishing pond right here in the basement."

"Very funny," he said, as he pushed more hose through the open window. "Junior, when you get that hose far enough away from the house; go to the truck and get my screw driver and pliers out of my tool box."

When I stood up and turned around to head for the truck, I bumped right into Mr. Wilson, the nosey, old man from down at the gas station.

"So this is the house your parents bought," he said, as he stooped over and looked through the basement window.

"As a matter of fact, it is Mr. Wilson; but I really don't have time to talk right now." I stepped around him and headed for the truck.

"It's Wilson... just call me Wilson," he corrected, as he followed close behind me.

"Okay...Wilson," I repeated, without turning around. The old man reached out and tapped me on the shoulder.

"Say, did I ever tell you about the folks that used to live here in this house?" he asked. I stopped and turned around.

"No, and I really don't have the..."

"Tony and Hazel Zinker were their names," Wilson continued, interrupting me. "They were some of the finest people in this town. Tony was a farmer. He worked nearly sixty acres and milked over thirty cows...twice a day! Then in 1943, a tornado swept through and took Tony's milking barn and the livestock. I always thought it odd, but he never did find those cows. After that, Hazel went to work for Tony's father, William Zinker, at the hardware in town."

"Look, Wilson," I said, trying to be polite. "I really have to..."

"Did I tell you William Zinker was Tony's father?" Wilson asked, interrupting me again. "He was once the richest man in Wannabe. He just about owned everything, including the lumber mill, train station, and the hardware. Old Mr. Zinker was the meanest, orneriest...he hated everyone, and everybody hated him. The story goes that he didn't trust banks, didn't trust people either."

Determined not to let Wilson keep me from my work, I went to the truck and grabbed my father's tools. The old man followed right behind me, picking up the story where he'd left off.

"William Zinker didn't like banks," he said, keeping in step with me. "Didn't like paper money either; he kept all his money in gold. Then one hot summer night, the old man up and died. To this day, no one has ever found that old man's hidden treasure." I stopped and spun around, just about knocking Wilson off his feet.

"Did you say hidden treasure?" I asked. Before he could answer, church bells began to ring off in the distance. And just like an obedient pet that had been called by his master, Wilson turned and headed for the driveway.

"Hear those bells, Junior?" he asked, looking back over his shoulder. "It's four o'clock, time for split pea soup." He took a few steps, then turned and looked back at me again. "Everyday at four o'clock I have pea soup," he said. Suddenly I forgot all about the tools my father had requested and followed after the old man.

"Is that all there is to the gold...I mean the story?" I asked trying to put on this 'I'm not too interested' act.

"No time, Junior," he said, as he continued down the driveway. "Got to get home to my soup. Would you like to join me?" I pondered the thought for a moment considering I wanted to hear more about this gold.

My mother leaned out the kitchen door a second time. "Junior, your father needs you!" she called out. I grabbed the tools and ran to the back of the house.

"What took you so long?" my father asked, his voice sounding a little irritated.

"Wilson, the old guy from the gas station stopped by for a visit," I said, as I handed the tools through the basement window.

"Wilson? What did he want?"

"I guess he just came by to welcome us to Wannabe."

For the next hour, I sat outside the basement window swatting at flies and mosquitoes while my father fought with the water pump in the basement. It seemed like every Tom, Dick, and Harry who drove by, slowed down and stared at me. I'm guessing people in this town are so bored with their own lives; they need to drive around and see what everybody else is doing.

"Junior!" my father called out again from the basement. "I need you to go to Zinker's Hardware and get me a new hose clamp."

"Did you just say Zinker's Hardware?" I asked.

"Yes," he said, putting his face right up to the basement window. "Now get a dollar from your mother; then get back here as fast as you can." I stood up and brushed the dust off my pants.

"Great!" I shouted, holding my hands up to the sky. "My first chance to get away from this prison!"

CHAPTER 2

COOKIES AND OTHER ASSORTED CHARACTERS

Armed with a crisp dollar bill in my pocket and directions to the hardware, I set out towards town. The directions turned out to be quite simple. From the old Zinker house located on Pine Street, I went west to the end of the street, turned left on Burnt Street and headed straight into town. Zinker's Hardware was located on the south side of the street next to the post office.

"Easy enough," I said to myself, as I walked out to the road.

As I got nearer to the corner of Pine and Burnt streets, I could hear a woman's voice. It was a powerful voice that echoed off the walls of the houses across the street. It reminded me of a big league baseball umpire or an army drill sergeant with one of those booming voices.

"Hey, you!" the voice thundered. "Young man!" I turned to see a woman hanging out a second story window. "Yes, you!" she said, as she pointed at me with her finger. "Please meet me at my front door!"

Seeing no reason why I shouldn't, I turned and walked up her sidewalk. Suddenly, the door flew open and out stepped a short, petite woman wearing a white dress partly covered by an apron with the words, "World's Best Baker", printed on the front. As I stared at her, she began rummaging through a purse the size of a suitcase, and I couldn't figure out if that big voice had actually come from that little woman.

"Here you go!" she said, handing me two dollars from the purse. She then reached into her apron pocket and handed me a warm cookie. "I want two loaves of bread and one half-gallon of milk! And if you get back before six o'clock, I'll give you another cookie!"

I took a deep breath and looked around. "Now, let me see if I've got this right, lady," I said, putting my hands on my hips. "You want me to get you two loaves of bread and one half-gallon of milk? And if I get back here by six o'clock, I get another warm cookie?"

She nodded and smiled. "Best cookies in town!" she said. She pulled a handful of cookies out of her apron pocket and paraded them past my nose. "Young man, I'll have you know, I'm going to be the next cookie baking champion of the world!"

"Is that so?" I inquired, as I looked around wondering if someone was playing a joke on me. She nodded as if to say yes. "Well, then, may I ask one question before I go?" I asked, as I sniffed my warm cookie. "Just where is the grocery store?"

The cookie lady, the name I gave her for lack of a better one, busted out into a full belly buster laugh. Her voice was so loud; I had to cover my ears. She grabbed me by my shoulders, spun me around and gave me a push. "That way, young man!" she shouted. She then turned and went back into the house, laughing every step of the way. Even with her door closed, I could still hear her laughing.

"Now, that was interesting," I said, as I stuffed the cookie into my mouth. I figured, what the hay, I could use another warm cookie.

Within a few minutes, I was standing at the corner of Burnt and Main streets in the middle of downtown Wannabe. Just off the corner to my right, I could see the train depot. It was a huge stone building with a wooden sign hanging out front. It had the words, "Wannabe Warrior, Village's Largest Newspaper," painted on it. Across the street, the hardware, post office and bank were all lined up side by side. I was surprised how deserted the downtown was on a Friday, considering it was around four o'clock in the afternoon. Except for two men sitting on a bench outside the hardware playing checkers, the town looked pretty much empty.

I stood there a minute studying the two strangers on the bench. One of the two men had a newspaper perched up in front of his face, while the other man's face was hidden by the shadow from a large, gray cowboy hat on his head. I figured they looked harmless enough, so I stepped off the curb and crossed the street. The man with the gray cowboy hat glanced at me as I walked towards them.

"Haven't seen you around town before," the man with the cowboy hat said, as he stood up and threw a smoldering cigarette butt out into the street. He stared at me silently as he lit up another. The man was rather tall with a small round beer gut that hung over his wide, western style leather belt. His face was unshaven, and his mustache looked as if it hadn't been trimmed in a year. "The name is Buck Porter," he said. "I'm the editor of the *Wannabe Warrior*, Wannabe's largest newspaper."

"The only newspaper in Wannabe!" mumbled the other man from behind the newspaper.

"My name is Junior, Junior Wolfe," I said, as I tried to get a look at the man who had his face covered.

"Ain't ever heard of you," the man snorted.

Buck Porter smiled. "Where are my manners, Junior? Mayor Moose Bronson, this here is Junior Wolfe. Junior, may I present the Honorable Moose Bronson, Wannabe's Mayor."

The man with the newspaper stood up and handed me a wrinkled business card. "Pleased to meet you, Junior Wolfe," he responded. Mayor Bronson was a short, round, stocky fellow dressed in a dirty, gray pin striped suit with tobacco stains that streaked down the middle of his dingy, white shirt. He wore wire-framed glasses that were so dirty; I could barely see his beady little eyes.

"Did you know our own Mayor Bronson is related to a famous man who signed the Declaration of Independence?" Buck Porter asked. "And soon, very soon, our mayor will be called to Washington to be a congressman!" The man with the gray hat reached over and slapped Mayor Bronson on the back congratulating him. When he did, brown tobacco juice dribbled out of his mouth and down onto his shirt. Buck

Porter broke out into laughter as the Mayor tried to wipe the stain off with his shirtsleeve.

"Why don't you tell the boy about your famous travels to the deepest jungles of Africa, Buck?" the Mayor asked, as he squinted to see through his dirty glasses. "And don't forget the part about how you got your head cut off by the natives!" he added.

"I didn't get my head cut off, you idiot!" Buck snapped. "I got my head shaved!" Buck took his hat off and hit Mayor Bronson on the head.

"Sorry, Buck!" The Mayor said, as he tried to keep from laughing. He covered his mouth as he began to wheeze and cough.

Buck pointed at the Mayor and began to laugh. "You sound just like a fat hyena!" he shouted.

I took a couple steps backward, hoping they wouldn't notice me leaving. I quickly turned and opened the hardware door and slipped inside.

"Talk about strange!" I said, half-whispering. I stared at the two men through the glass for a moment.

Zinker's Hardware was about as small-town as it gets. Everything you could imagine was all crammed into narrow walkways and tall shelves. No one was tending the counter, so I decided to take a short tour. The wooden floors squeaked as I walked up and down the aisles. Above some tool racks, hanging on the back wall, was a large oil painting of an older man. The way he was dressed, it reminded me of somebody from the civil war days.

"That's my great-grandfather, William Zinker," a quiet voice from behind me said. I turned around to see a young man a few years older than myself looking up at the painting. He was tall and thin with dark, wavy hair. He was dressed in jeans and a red flannel shirt; and a clerk's apron was draped around his neck.

"I see you've met our mayor and Buck, the newspaper man, outside," he said. "My name is Ralph Zinker."

I reached out, and we shook hands. "I'm Junior Wolfe," I replied. I looked past Ralph's shoulder wondering if the Mayor and Buck were still outside. "Is it my imagination or is everybody in this town strange?" I asked. Ralph laughed.

"Yep, just about everybody," he said. "But those two outside…they're the worst!"

Ralph pulled a pencil and pad from his apron pocket. "So, Junior, what can I get for you?" he asked.

"I need a hose clamp, two loaves of bread, and one half-gallon of milk," I said, as I pulled some money out of my pocket.

Ralph smiled. "Seems like an odd combination, but simple enough," he said. "Over here is the plumbing aisle. What's the hose clamp for?" he asked.

"My parents bought a house over on Pine Street, and it has water in the basement. My father wants to pump out the water, but he needs a new clamp to connect the hose to the pump."

Ralph's eyebrows went up. "I remember my father telling me that the Wolfe family bought my grandparents' house."

"Tony and Hazel Zinker were your grandparents?" I asked.

"Yep," Ralph said with a smile. "My father got the farm when they passed away. Your parents have a lot of work to do on that old place, Junior."

I nodded my head in agreement. "That's for sure!" I said.

Ralph looked around to see if there was anybody else in the hardware. "What do you know about the Zinker family?" Ralph asked, in a whisper.

"Well, not that I asked, but Wilson stopped by and told me about your great-grandfather's missing gold."

Ralph surveyed the hardware one more time. "Junior, I need your help. Can I show you something?"

I followed Ralph to a storage room at the back of the hardware where he closed the door behind us. He then pulled an old book out of a drawer and plopped it down on the desk.

"This was my great-grandfather's last business journal before he died," Ralph said, as he opened it up. "Notice anything different about this journal?"

He handed me the dust-covered book, and I quickly flipped through the pages. "Well, there's a page missing," I said, handing him the journal back.

"I think that missing page tells where the gold is hidden," Ralph said excitedly. "And that page may be somewhere in my grandfather's house! In your house, Junior…and you can help me find it!"

Suddenly Ralph pushed the journal back into the desk drawer and locked it. "There's someone in the hardware!" he whispered. He opened the door slowly and peeked out. "It's Mayor Bronson and Buck Porter," he said, before hurrying out the door to meet them. I stayed out of sight and watched Ralph and the two men from a crack in the wooden door.

"What can I get for you Mr. Mayor and Mr. Porter," Ralph asked, as he nervously glanced over his shoulder in the direction of the storage room.

"Where's your Cold Star chewing tobacco?" Mayor Bronson asked, as he adjusted his dirty glasses.

Ralph went behind the counter and grabbed the chewing tobacco off a shelf. "Anything else?" he asked.

"Give me a pack of cigarette papers," Buck added, "and put it on the Mayor's tab."

"But, Buck," the Mayor said, protesting in a whiney voice. "My wife told me not to…"

"Come on, Moose…be a man!" Buck snapped back, cutting the Mayor off in the middle of his sentence.

"Is that it?" Ralph asked again.

Mayor Bronson and Buck turned and left the hardware without answering. Ralph waited for the front door to close before signaling the all clear.

"They're gone!" Ralph called out; I joined him at the front counter.

"Do you think they overheard us in the back room?" I asked.

"No telling," Ralph answered.

I looked at my watch. "I've got to get going, Ralph. If I don't get back soon, my pop is going to kill me."

Ralph packed the two loaves of bread, the half-gallon of milk, and the hose clamp in a bag. "There you go," he said. "That food should do you 'til tomorrow."

"The bread and milk are not for me," I said, pulling the bag close to my chest. "They're for the cookie lady."

"Who?" Ralph asked, with a puzzled look on his face.

"Some lady on Pine Street asked me to get her these things. She said that if I was back before six o'clock, I'd get a cookie."

Ralph laughed. "That's Mrs. Harman," he said. "She's loud, but she makes the best cookies in the world."

I shook the bag. "First stop, the cookie lady's house!" I announced, as I headed for the door.

Outside the hardware, Buck and the Mayor were waiting for me.

"Well, well, what do you have in the bag, kid?" Mayor Bronson demanded, as he stepped in front of me.

"Food," I said, as I opened the bag.

Buck leaned forward and looked inside. "What were you and Ralph doing in the back room?" Buck asked, as he folded his arms.

I wrinkled my nose and turned away. "I'd tell you but…" I paused. "You really need to do something about your breath, Mr. Porter."

Mayor Bronson busted out laughing, spitting tobacco juice out of his mouth again.

"Look, kid, we know what you two were talking about!" Buck said in an accusing voice.

"We have ways to make you talk," Mayor Bronson chimed in.

"I don't know what you two are talking about!" I said, trying to sound innocent.

"What's that noise?" Buck interrupted. He turned and looked toward the west end of town.

Mayor Bronson stepped out into the street and looked in the same direction. "Buck, its Friday!" he said nervously, as he pulled out his pocket watch.

Suddenly, a man and woman rushed out of the post office and ran down the street. 'Closed for business' signs appeared in several storefront windows, and even a dog, sensing some kind of danger, ran for cover.

From far off in the distance, I could hear this loud rumble and with each passing moment, it grew louder and louder. Buck and Mayor Bronson had this look on their faces, like the death angel himself would be arriving at any moment.

"Did you say Friday, Mayor?" Buck asked in a weak voice. "I just remembered something. I've got to work on a breaking story for the newspaper!" Buck stepped off the sidewalk and started across the street.

"Hey, wait for me!" Mayor Bronson shouted, as he chased after him. "I'm not facing those Rustler boys all by myself!"

"Who are the Rustler boys?" I called out, trying to get Mayor Bronson to answer.

"Billy and Jesse Rustler," the Mayor said, in a low voice. "Jesse is the fat one with a beard. Billy is the one with a scar on his face."

Buck and the Mayor were halfway across the street when a beat-up construction dump truck roared into town. It slowed down and made a wide u-turn stopping right in front of the village bar. Buck and the Mayor froze in their tracks and watched as two scruffy looking men got out of the truck. They were covered in dirt from their heads down to their dirty boots and when they laughed and slapped each other on the back, big puffs of dust came off of their clothes.

Jesse Rustler turned and went into the bar while Billy walked out into the middle of the street. He slowly turned until he faced Buck and Mayor Bronson; it reminded me of a Wild West showdown.

Buck and the Mayor whispered back and forth as they stood there, frozen like statues. Jesse Rustler returned with two bottles of beer and joined his brother in the middle of the street. They guzzled their beer down in seconds then tossed the empty bottles up against a building, where they smashed into a thousand pieces. At the sound of the bottles shattering, Buck and the Mayor made a break for the other side of the street.

"Stop right there!" Billy ordered, his deep voice echoing up and down the deserted street. The two frightened men obeyed and skidded to a stop.

"Where do you boys think you're going?" Jesse asked, in a demanding voice. Buck fumbled for words.

"As a matter of fact, we were on our way to meet you," he said, in an unconvincing voice. The two men at the other end of the street let out a big belly laugh.

"It wouldn't be very good manners to skip out on our poker game now would it, boys?" Billy asked, as he shifted a big wad of tobacco from one side of his mouth to the other before spitting half of the disgusting stuff on the street. Buck and the Mayor whimpered then reluctantly joined the two men. I watched as they followed behind like whipped puppies, before finally disappearing into the bar. After what I'd just witnessed, I was now more convinced than ever that everyone in this town was really crazy. I crossed the street and headed for the cookie lady's house. Mrs. Harman was waiting on the front porch when I arrived and, satisfied that I had held up my part of the bargain, handed over another warm cookie. I quickly stuffed it in my mouth thinking Ralph had it right; this lady really did make good cookies. As I headed back to the old Zinker farm, I glanced at my watch. *I've been gone for just over an hour; my parents will think I've run away.* Suddenly it occurred to me. *Wait a minute*, I thought, slowing my pace. *Maybe that's not such a bad idea!*

My parents had put aside their busy bee activities and were sitting on the side porch waiting for me when I returned to the old homestead. "We were just about to send a search party out when we spotted you coming down the street," my mother said, as she handed me a warm glass of lemonade.

"So, did you get to the hardware store?" my father asked. I nodded.

"Here you go, Pop," I said, as I handed him the hose clamp.

"Was Mr. Zinker's son, Ralph, working at the hardware today?" my mother asked.

"As a matter of fact, I did get a chance to meet Ralph, and a few other interesting people in this town." I smiled and wiggled my eyebrows. My mother looked at me in surprise.

"What other interesting people?" she asked. I began to pace back and forth as if I was trying to think of just the right words.

"Just where do I begin?" I asked, as I folded my arms.

"Oh, yes, first, I met Wilson…. he's the man from the gas station. He eats pea soup every day and likes to tell stories. I also met a lady who lives on our street and has a voice like a drill sergeant. She is so loud; her voice could break the sound barrier. She indiscriminately gives money to strangers and hands out cookies in exchange for milk and bread. Oh, and she wants to be the cookie queen of the world. Then, I had the privilege of meeting Wannabe's mayor while in town. He thinks he's famous, and he wants to be a congressman. His name is Moose, and he laughs like a hyena. He dresses like a cheap salesman, and he spits tobacco on himself. I'm not quite sure, but I think he's the village idiot. I also met Buck Porter, the village's newspaper reporter, who claims to be a world-wide traveler. The story goes that he had his head cut off while in Africa, and he's still alive to tell about it. Last but not least, I got to see Billy and Jesse Rustler, the town bullies. They think they're Billy and Jesse James, and every Friday they come into town, play poker, throw beer bottles, and generally bust up the place. This two-bit town sure has its share of weirdoes!"

When I finished, my parents were staring at me as if I'd just told some kind of fantasy story. Unfortunately, there was no look of fear or panic on their faces. No one was screaming or hurrying to pack suitcases and run back to the city.

"Oh, well," I said, as I shrugged my shoulders. "I had a feeling you wouldn't believe me."

"It's not that we don't believe you, Junior," my mother said, while still looking at my father. She turned and put her hand on my shoulder. "It's just…well; you do have a vivid imagination."

CHAPTER 3

AN UNSUAL WELCOME

While my parents were busy with their obsession…working on that excuse for a house, my plan was to search every square inch of the place and find that missing journal page. My strategy was simple. I'd start on the first floor, going room-to-room, closet-to-closet, and loose floorboard to loose floorboard. Then, I'd move up to the second floor, finishing up with the attic…not that I'm thrilled about attics. I've heard bats are known to hang out in attics, especially old attics, and they're not exactly my favorite little winged animal. I spent a moment stretching as if I were preparing to run an important race.

"Ready or not, here I come!" I said, as I grabbed the handle on the screen door. "If I find that journal page, which will lead me to the lost gold, we'll be out of here and back to civilization before Wilson can say, 'pea-soup'."

For the next several hours I did a thorough search of the house from top to bottom…except for the basement. …There was no way I was going into that wet basement. Unfortunately, after searching every crack and hole in that old house, I couldn't find any missing journal page.

"Oh, well," I said, kicking a piece of loose plaster across the floor. "So much for that idea. Of course, this means spending at least one night in this forsaken old dump. Great! I guess I'll go back into town tomorrow and give Ralph the bad news." I took my things upstairs to the room I had been arbitrarily assigned, and after having a cold sandwich and warm milk for dinner, I went back upstairs and settled in for the night.

It was exactly two o'clock when it happened. And how did I know it was two o'clock? My father, while in his 'I've got to fix everything in this house tonight' mood, revived a long silent, dusty, old grandfather clock that stood in the corner of the living room. So that, every hour on the hour, the chimes rang loud and clear, reminding me that I was, or at least had been, asleep. So back to what happened at two o'clock…bats! One moment, only silence. The next, a hundred little swishing wings were going to and fro around my room. It was as if I was in one of those horror movies. You know, where if you stick your head out from under the covers, a bat lands on your neck and sucks your blood! While I lay there covered up, unable to move a muscle, a huge bat landed on the bed. It scurried across the top of the covers coming towards my head. I knew if I didn't do something quickly, I would be found in the morning by my parents…dead, and drained of all my blood. I took a deep breath and slid my hand out from underneath the covers and reached over and turned on my table lamp.

If I'm going to go down fighting, I want to see the eyes of my enemies! I thought. When I peeled the covers away from my face, a fat gray cat was sitting calmly on the edge of the bed just staring at me. Before I could say a word, a bat swooped past and with one lighting-quick strike, that cat slapped that bat right out of the air, pounced on it then ran out of the room. I don't know what happened to the other ninety-nine bats that were in that room, but I'm guessing they didn't want to be around when that cat came back.

Later…sometime after midnight and before sunrise on Saturday morning, I was suddenly awakened by a loud freight train. Again, like the day before, the whole house began to rattle and shake as the train rumbled by. The upstairs jail...I mean, the bedroom where I was forced to sleep, had this old, metal-framed bed on wheels. The vibration from the train transformed this antique bed from what I thought was an immovable object into a nightmarish carnival ride. It rolled back and forth around the room like a roller coaster, and I was sure it was going to crash through the window sending me tumbling to my premature death. Then, as I shouted out my last prayer, fully expecting to go before my maker, the bed came to a stop, resting exactly in the same position as before. I threw the covers off my face and wiped the sweat off my forehead. I looked at my knuckles; they were white from grabbing on for dear life. I sat up and breathed a sigh of relief. *What is this, some kind of haunted house?*

I quickly jumped out of bed and went to the window, wondering if the rest of the house was still in one piece. I listened intently for a moment; except for a few chirping birds, it was dead quiet…at least for those few seconds. Then, like a blast of a foghorn, I heard a booming voice coming from somewhere outside.

I recognize that voice, I thought, pulling the curtains back. *It's the cookie lady!* Putting my nose against the dirty window, I could see her and another lady standing in the driveway talking to my parents. I strained to open the window but had no such luck. And wanting desperately to hear what they were talking about, I raced downstairs and returned with my father's crowbar. With a little persuasion, the stubborn window finally popped open; and I leaned my head out just in time to see the two ladies waving good-bye. Feeling completely frustrated, I threw the crowbar down on the bed and sat down. The worn curtains hanging on the window began to sway back and forth and the smell of fresh brewed coffee and cooked bacon filled my room. I took a deep breath, it instantly made me hungry. I figured if I got dressed and went downstairs, I could interrogate my parents and find out what the cookie lady was doing here. When I walked into the kitchen, I found my father sitting at the old kitchen table reading the *Wannabe Warrior* newspaper. My mother was standing at the stove turning over sizzling bacon and stirring scrambled eggs in a pan. The way they acted, it was as if they had been living here forever.

"You two could be Tony and Hazel Zinker the way you look in this kitchen," I said, as I sat down. "Hey, Ma Zinker, may I have some o' those vittles you all are cooking?" I asked.

"A bunch of vittles, coming right up!" my mother said, playing along.

"What's the price on hogs today, Pa?" I asked, as I got a plate and handed it to my mother. My father put down the paper and stared hard at me.

"Better give all of us some of that strong coffee you've made Ma, 'cause there's some very interestin' stuff written about us in this here paper."

"What's in the paper about us?" my mother asked, looking very surprised. She sat down beside my father.

"This article, or should I say fairy tale, is written by a man named Buck Porter," he informed us, as he began to read out loud.

THE VILLAGE OF WANNABE WELCOMES NEWEST RESIDENT

Mr. Jonathon Zinker of Pine Street, one of Wannabe's leading citizens, sold his grandparents' farm, or what's left of it, to a family from the Detroit area. The Wolfe family, consisting of Mr. and Mrs. Michael Wolfe, along with their son Junior, moved in and took possession of the dilapidated property this past Friday. Mr. Wolfe, an unemployed woodworker, was given a job at the Zinker Lumber Mill and information has been given, yet not confirmed, that Mrs. Wolfe has no measurable skills and no doubt will be a stay-at-home wife. It was also reported, but not confirmed, that Junior Wolfe was removed from a school in Detroit for some unknown reason and, therefore, will be attending Wannabe High School this coming fall.

My mother jumped up out of her chair, as if a snake had bitten her. "Why, that no good!" she said, as she marched around the room.

"Buck Porter owns the *Wannabe Warrior* newspaper, and I wouldn't trust him any farther than I could throw him!"

I said, as I reached for a pitcher of milk at the far end of the table.

"Why would anyone print such a story?" my mother asked angrily.

"They think I know something about William Zinker's hidden gold!"

"What are you talking about?" my father asked, as he reached for his coffee.

I told my parents about Ralph showing me his grandfather's journal and the missing page. I told them that Ralph was convinced the missing page was hidden somewhere in our house. I also told them about Mayor Bronson and Buck Porter coming into the hardware and spying on Ralph and me and then only moments later, cornering me outside. They claimed I knew where the gold might be hidden.

"'We have ways to make you talk,' Mayor Bronson said to me. If it weren't for the Rustlers coming into town, I'd still be there being pushed around by those two!"

My father stiffened up in his chair as if he were upset.

My mother walked over to my father and put her hand on his shoulder. "We have to do something about this, Michael!" she demanded. "They have no business picking on Junior."

My father looked at my mother then looked at his watch. "Look, Dear," he said, as he gathered up his dishes. "I don't have to remind you we are outsiders in this little town. I've got to work with these people and now is not the time to go looking for trouble." He got up from the table and moved towards the door. "This unemployed woodworker has to get to work," he said. My mother turned and followed him to the door.

"You go on to work dear," my mother said, as she kissed him on the cheek. "This 'brainless blond' will stay at home and do some meaningless house cleaning." He smiled slightly then went out the door.

My mother watched my father drive away before getting a fresh cup of coffee and returning to the table. "Tell me more about this missing journal page," she asked, as she settled down into her chair.

"Remember yesterday when I was helping pop with the water in the basement?" I asked. My mother nodded. "Well, that's when Wilson, that old guy from the gas station, showed up. He started talking about Ralph's grandparents, Tony and Hazel Zinker, and how they were farmers. He talked about Ralph's great-grandfather, William Zinker, and how he hated banks. Wilson said that one day William Zinker up and died and to this day no one has ever found the old man's gold.

Then yesterday, while at the hardware, Ralph showed me his great-grandfather's journal with the missing page. He thinks that page, which may hold the secret to where the gold is hidden, is somewhere in this house."

Suddenly, my mother's eyes grew very large. She stood up and hurried into the other room. She returned a moment later holding a worn piece of paper in her hand. "I found this paper in the dining room closet," she said, holding it up. "It was hidden behind a loose board."

When she set it down on the table, right away I recognized it as the missing page. "Do you know what this means?" I asked, as I grabbed the page. "This may tell us where the gold is hidden. I began reading the journal page out loud.

July 1st, 1928. Three days until Wannabe's Independence Day festival. I am still waiting for the construction work between the two buildings to be completed. I have found using out-of-town workers has its difficulties as well as its advantages. The purchase of ten new rock picks and shovels this week were unexpected. Eddie has been given the brass key with the family seal which opens the strong box as well as the heavy doors. The wagon and the strong box have been prepared to carry the heavy cargo. The fireworks display at the park, paid for by the Zinker family, was a brilliant idea. This will insure that the downtown will be empty during the transfer of the goods.

Quickly realizing the journal page didn't tell where the gold was located, I tossed it down on the table. "So much for it telling where the gold is hidden," I grumbled.

"I wonder what construction he's talking about?" my mother asked, as she picked up the paper and studied it. "And why would William Zinker try to get everybody away from town for that evening?" She set the journal down and slid it back over to me. "I'll bet if you and Ralph put your heads together, you'll figure it out."

Thinking that wasn't such a bad idea, I jumped up and turned towards the door. "I'll go right now," I said.

Before I could take a step, my mother reached out and grabbed me and spun me around. "Wait a minute, you," she said, pulling me back down into my chair. "It's a good idea, but not right now."

"Why, what's going on?" I asked.

"I'm going to have some guests over this morning, and I need you here," she said. My mother pushed in her chair and started clearing off the table. She had this nervous look about her, as if she was trying really hard to act normal.

"All right, Lady, spill your guts!" I said, as I folded my arms.

She tried to smile again as she fumbled for words. "Well, you see, I met these two ladies from down the street, and I invited them for tea."

"Is that who you and pop were talking to this morning?" I asked, not that I hadn't already figured that out.

My mother nodded. "Mrs. Zinker, Ralph's mother, and Mrs. Harman will be coming over this morning. It's sort of a 'welcome to Wannabe' visit."

"Okay, I'm listening," I said, as I unfolded my arms.

"Anyway, Mrs. Harman's daughter is coming; and I was wondering if…"

"Oh, no you don't!" I snapped, interrupting my mother. "I'm not babysitting some little snotty nosed kid from down the street!"

"She's not a little kid!" my mother snapped back. "She's the same age as you. Her name is Becky, and she's also a friend of Ralph Zinker." My mother pointed to the journal page lying on the table. "Maybe she knows something about the missing gold; it can't hurt to find out."

I stood up and paced across the room, thinking it over for a moment. If I could get information out of this Becky that could lead me to the lost gold, then I could get out of this two-bit town. "All right, I guess it can't hurt," I said. "I'll do it but on one condition."

"What's that," my mother asked.

"If the cookie lady brings cookies, I want my share."

My mother busted out laughing. "I promise I'll save some cookies for you! Now that that's settled, your father wants you to start cleaning out the barn."

"What…that old barn?" I asked, pointing outside.

"Yes, that old barn. Now go!" My mother turned me around and walked me to the door.

"Great, just what I wanted to do today!" I said, in a sarcastic voice. "Play farmer in the dump in this lousy little town!"

CHAPTER 4

THE BEGINNING OF A NEW FRIENDSHIP

For a few moments, I just stood in front of the old barn surveying the situation. Two large barn doors faced the driveway, and each door had a long wooden pole leaning against it holding it closed. I lifted a pole off one of the doors and pushed it aside; the door swung all the way open. I slowly stepped inside; the place smelled like dry cow manure and stale hay.

"This barn is a mess!" I muttered. The floor was cluttered knee deep with everything from old tractor tires to worn out furniture. I stumbled and kicked my way to the center of the barn and flopped down on a bale of hay. This was not how I spent my weekends in the city! Kids in the city cut the grass or washed cars but never had to clean out smelly barns. A cooing sound caught my attention as a pair of doves flew into the barn through an open window, landing on a beam above the hayloft.

"Hayloft!" I exalted. "Haylofts are a great place to hide!" I looked around and spotted a ladder in the center of the barn going up through a square hole in the upper floor. The temptation was just too great, and I didn't stop until I was at the top of the ladder. *I'll lure the cookie lady's daughter over to the barn, swing down and scare the life out of her...She'll scream, run home, and that will be that!*

Up in the hayloft, two smaller wooden doors faced the front of the barn. I unlatched the doors and pushed them open. Protruding out of the wall above the doors was a wooden beam, and a heavy rope hung down from this beam.

This is great! I thought, surveying my vantage point. I reached out and grabbed the rope and waited for my victim to arrive. As I waited, I imagined what the cookie lady's daughter looked like. If she's anything like her mother, she'll have a voice louder than Niagara Falls. She'll probably have braces on her teeth, and she'll spit all over me every time she opens her big mouth. She'll no doubt have cookies stuffed in her dirty overall pockets and constantly be eating them one after another like candy.

I sat down in the hay and waited for the ladies to come up the driveway. I had no sooner settled in when they arrived, walking directly to the side porch where my mother was waiting to greet them.

"Junior!" my mother called out. "Becky is here!"

I slipped back out of view, so they couldn't see me. "I'm up in the hay loft!" I called out. When I peeked over the edge, I could see a girl coming towards the barn. I tightened my grip on the rope, gave a yell and jumped. My little surprise didn't turn out exactly like I'd imagined. When I jumped, the rope dug into my hands causing excruciating pain, which in turn, caused me to prematurely let go. Needless to say, gravity took over; I fell like a rock all the way to the ground. The impact with an immovable object called Earth knocked the wind out of me, and I lay there for a moment struggling to breathe.

The cookie lady's daughter ran up to me and stood looking down at me. "What was that?" she asked, as she reached down to help me up.

I staggered to my feet, still gasping for air. "I'll bet you've never seen that trick before," I said, almost whispering. I looked away, feeling embarrassed at making an idiot of myself.

She smiled. "You're right; I don't ever recall seeing that done before...at least on purpose." She put her hand out. "Hi, I'm Becky Harman," she said. I reached out and shook her hand.

"Glad to meet you," I said. "My name is Junior Wolfe." Becky was nothing like I'd expected. Even though she was wearing overalls, I could tell she was tall and slender. And I couldn't help but notice her long, wavy auburn hair and hazel eyes.

"What were you doing up in the loft?" Becky asked, as she brushed her hair out of her eyes.

"I wasn't practicing so I could join the circus, if that's what you're wondering," I said sarcastically. Becky laughed at my response. "If you must know, my parents asked me to start cleaning out the barn; and I noticed the loft, and well, the rest is history."

"Are you related to the Zinkers?" Becky asked.

"No," I snapped at her. "We're outsiders! Didn't you read the story that Porter guy wrote about my family in his stupid paper?"

Becky nodded. "I heard my parents read it out loud at the kitchen table this morning," she said. "I think it was shameful."

"Most of it was lies, you know," I said, fanning my burning hands back and forth. "But having met Buck Porter, and Mayor Bronson, the village idiot, in town yesterday, I guess I shouldn't have been surprised."

Becky busted out laughing again. "You're funny, Junior!" she said, as she reached for my hands. "I know what would be good for those rope burns…follow me." She turned and headed for the back yard.

"Where are we going?" I asked, following after her.

"To the stream out back," she said. We walked down a narrow path that weaved in and around some thick weeds and brier bushes.

"I didn't know there was a stream back here," I said, as I tried to keep up.

Becky suddenly stopped, and I looked over her shoulder. We were standing at an old wooden bridge. The stream looked to be about twenty-five feet wide and three or four feet deep. I was surprised to see how clear the water looked.

Becky bent down and touched the water. "Come on, Junior, the water is warm!" she said, as she splashed the water on me. When I sat down and touched the water, dozens of minnows scattered in all directions. "Keep your hands in the water; it has healing powers," Becky said, as she smiled at me. "When I was young, I used to pretend this stream came from a magical fountain in a far-off kingdom. I would throw a hand full of wild flowers into the water and make wishes as they floated down stream." Becky splashed at her reflection in the water.

"Did your wishes come true?" I asked, as I tried to catch a minnow.

"Some," Becky said, as she pushed her small framed glasses up on her nose.

"So, Junior," she said, looking into my eyes. "If you could wish for something, what would it be?" She stared at me, waiting for an answer.

I stirred the water until my reflection became distorted. "I wish I could get out of this crummy little town and go back home!" I said, hitting the water with my fist.

"Hey!" Becky shouted as she jumped up. "I know just what you need!" She put her knee in the middle of my back and gave me a push. "You need to cool off!"

Before I could react, I was tumbling head first into the water. Becky laughed as I came up from under the water gasping for air. I just stood there in the water for what seemed like an eternity before she reached down and offered to help pull me out. "Grab on," she said.

"Thanks," I said. "I thought you'd never ask." I reached for her hand, took a firm grip and gave a quick tug. She let out a scream as she flew over my shoulder and landed in the water.

"Hey, you did that on purpose!" she shouted, as she popped up out of the water like a fishing bobber. She reached out and punched me in the arm. "Here," she said, splashing water in my face. "You need a bath." I took my turn splashing her back then teased her repeatedly about her dripping wet hair.

"Hey," Becky said, pointing to some dandelions growing along the edge of the stream, "let's make a wish."

"Why?" I asked, thinking it was a silly.

"Because it's fun," she said. "Now go get us some flowers before I beat you up." I laughed at the thought of Becky trying to beat me up as I waded to the edge of the stream. I picked several of the small dandelions and returned, handing them to her.

"My wish is going to be that you won't beat me up," I said, showing her my best puppy-dog face.

"Everybody knows your wish won't come true if you tell anybody before you put the flowers into the water…City Boy!" Becky tossed the flowers into the water, and we watched as they floated down stream. As the very last flowers disappeared from site, the sun broke through the clouds sending warm rays up and down the stream.

Suddenly, as if the brightness of the sun had made us come to our senses, making us realize how silly we both were acting, we climbed back up onto the bridge to dry off. Becky tipped her head back and stared up into the sky as huge white clouds floated by.

"Okay, now what do we do?" I asked, as I watched puddles of water collect under me.

"We change!" Becky said, as she jumped up and punched me in the arm again. "I'll run home, change and come back. Then we'll go up to the gas station for a cold soda." Becky pushed me aside and ran back up towards the house. "Meet me at the railroad tracks in fifteen minutes!" she called out.

I reluctantly went back up to the house knowing all those ladies would be in the kitchen. I wasn't quite sure what I was going to tell them. I stepped through the doorway and hurried across the room, hoping my wet shoes wouldn't make that loud squishing noise. When the talking suddenly stopped, I knew I was in trouble.

"Junior," my mother said, in a low voice. "Why are you soaking wet?" I turned around and smiled nervously. All three women were staring intently at me as if I'd just committed some kind of crime.

"I suppose you're all wondering why I'm wet," I said, looking down at my wet shoes. "I accidentally got pushed… I mean, I fell into the stream, and I hope you don't mind me coming in to change clothes."

Mrs. Harman got up and looked out the window. "Where's my Becky?" she asked, turning to me and giving a hard stare.

"She went home for something," I said. "She'll be back in a few minutes." I smiled my, I'm innocent smile and headed for the living room. "Oh," I said, turning around. "If you ladies don't mind, Becky and I would like to go up to the gas station for a cold soda…my treat of course."

There was a brief silence, before Mrs. Harman finally gave her approval. "Just to the gas station and back mind you!" she said, her booming voice rattling the dishes on the table.

"Thank you, ma'am," I called out, as I hurried upstairs to change.

Becky was good to her word. She was waiting for me at the railroad tracks when I arrived. "What did you tell your mom about being wet?" Becky asked, as we began walking along the edge of the road.

"Just the simple fact that I fell into the stream," I said.

"Did you tell them about me getting wet?" she asked with a smile.

"I seemed to have forgotten that part," I said. "But, I did ask permission for you and me to get a soda."

"Good job, Junior!" Becky said, reaching out and punching me in the arm.

"Do you punch everybody in the arm?" I asked, as I gave Becky a little push. She flipped her hair out of her eyes and looked at me.

"Not everybody," she said. "Just my friends."

From the time she'd arrived with her mother, I had been itching to ask Becky what she knew about the missing Zinker gold. Thinking, *there's no time like the present*, I just blurted it out. "What do you know about the missing Zinker gold?" I turned and grabbed at some wild flowers at the edge of the road, pretending it didn't matter if she answered.

She stopped and looked at me in surprise. "Whom have you been talking to?" she asked.

"Well, there's this old guy, Wilson, who came to the house yesterday."

"Wilson," Becky said, repeating his name. "I should have known. What did he tell you?"

"Some story about Tony and Hazel Zinker. He talked about Tony's father, William Zinker, and about the missing gold."

"Did he tell you that Tony Zinker's grandson, Ralph, and about half the people in this town are looking for that gold?" Becky asked. She stopped and put her hands on her hips. I turned and faced her.

"I met Ralph yesterday at the hardware," I said. "Ralph showed me the journal, and he asked me to help him find the missing page from the journal."

Becky stared hard at me. "Wow!" she exclaimed. "I'm really surprised at Ralph, him not knowing you and all."

"I think he did it because of that old dump," I said, pointing back at the old Zinker house. "And when we get back, there's something my Mom found that I want to show you."

When we arrived at the gas station, Mr. Stubbs, the station attendant, was outside exercising. He appeared to be lifting toilets over his head. When he noticed us, he stopped and waved.

Becky turned to me and whispered. "Don't say anything. Just let me do the talking."

"That's all right with me," I said, whispering back. Not that I knew what she was talking about.

"Hello, Miss Becky," Mr. Stubbs said, in a soft voice. Becky reached out and grabbed me by the arm.

"Mr. Stubbs, may I present to you my friend, Junior."

"Howdy, young man!" he said, as he put his hand out.

"Glad to meet you," I said, reaching out and shaking his hand.

"What do you think of my weights?" he asked, looking rather proud of his handy work. The big man with the bald head had somehow attached two toilets for weights at both ends of a heavy steel bar. It was the strangest set of dumb bells I'd ever seen. "Took me near a month to figure out how to fasten all of this together," he said.

I looked at Becky and then turned back to Mr. Stubbs. "Why toilets?" I asked, trying my best not to laugh.

"I collect them," he said, with a big smile on his face. "I want to build me a toilet museum one of these days right here in Wannabe. I can just see it now," he said, waving his hands in the air. "I'll have a building full of rows and rows of toilets, each in its own little stall. People will come from miles around just to see and use my toilets."

"Use them?" I asked, as I looked at Becky out of the corner of my eye.

"Hey, want to see the rest of my toilet collection?" He pointed to a pile of toilets at the side of the gas station.

"Sorry, Mr. Stubbs," Becky said, turning to me. "I think I hear my mother calling me." Becky leaned over and whispered in my ear.

"Let's get our soda and get out of here."

"Suit yourselves," Mr. Stubbs said, as he went back to lifting his toilets over his head. "Next time you come, Junior, I'll show you the rest of my toilet collection!" I waved without looking back.

When we arrived back to the house, my mother and her two visitors were on the porch talking.

"Come on, Becky, time to go!" Mrs. Harman shouted, her voice booming across the yard.

I turned to Becky. "You can't go now; I've got to show you something!"

Becky called back to her mother. "Okay, Mom!" She turned back to me. "Tomorrow, after church," she said. "Bring whatever you have and meet me at Ralph's house."

"And where's that?" I asked, holding my hands in the air.

"Right across the street from my house," she said, pointing down the street. "It's the tall white house with wood pillars on the front porch."

"Come, Becky!" Her mother said, as she walked past. "And, Junior, thank you again for the milk and bread!"

Becky looked at me with a puzzled look on her face. "What was that about?" she asked in a whisper.

"I'll tell you tomorrow," I whispered back. "Hey, and if you can, bring some of your mom's cookies tomorrow," I added.

Becky punched me again. "What is it about boys and cookies?" she asked, shaking her head.

"Junior!" my mother called from the house. "Mrs. Harman left something for you!"

"What is it?" I asked, as I walked up the driveway. Then I remembered…"Cookies!" I shouted. I ran all the way to the kitchen. Inside, I found a single cookie left on a big plate. I grabbed for the cookie and sat down. I looked at my mother and gave her this, where are the rest of the cookies, look.

"Sorry there weren't more," she said, "We got a little carried away." She came and sat down across from me.

"That's okay," I said, finishing off the one cookie. "We're getting together at Ralph's tomorrow afternoon and I asked Becky to bring some more."

My mother laughed. "Sounds like you've made a friend." She began tapping her fingers on the table as if she was trying to remember something. "Before you get back to the barn, I wanted to tell you something," she said. "We've been invited by the Harman and Zinker families to visit their church tomorrow."

"It's all right with me," I said, as I got up for a glass of milk. "I hope pop doesn't expect the barn to be cleaned out in one day. Not with one hundred years worth of stuff packed in there!"

My mother got up and began clearing off the table. "Thomas Zinker told your father you could keep anything you find in that barn. You never know, you may find something of great value."

“In that old barn?” I asked, sounding a little sarcastic. “I don’t think so!” I gulped down the last of my milk then walked to the door.

“Ma’am,” I said, as I turned around. “If I don’t come back by dark, send in the troops!” I saluted and pushed the screen door open.

“Hey, Private,” my mother said, as she grabbed a broom and tossed it to me. “You’re going to need this.”

“Thank you, Ma’am,” I said, slightly bowing. “You’re much too kind to this lowly stable boy.”

CHAPTER 5

STRANGE DISCOVERY!

Carrying the broom resting over my shoulder like a gun, I marched across the yard. I came to an abrupt stop in front of the weathered barn doors and stood at attention. I considered my mother's words for a moment, wondering what strange things waited to be discovered under all that junk. Although I wasn't thrilled about cleaning out the barn, I did have this odd feeling that I just might find something that would point the way to the Zinker gold.

Taking a deep breath, I grabbed the barn doors, throwing them open with all my might. I planted my feet and squared my shoulders ready to face the enemy. Lying before me was the biggest, most massive heap of junk I'd ever seen. It looked like a crouching beast, ready to pounce on me at any moment. I raised my broom…I mean weapon in defense.

"You're no match for me beast!" I shouted. I moved slowly to the left, then slowly to the right, trying to gain an advantage. I spied a short handled pitchfork hanging on the wall just inside the door. Making a split-second decision, I dropped the broom and lunged for the pointed weapon. As I grabbed the pitchfork, a breeze suddenly swept through the drafty old barn, sending dry straw swirling across the floor like tumble weeds. I raised my weapon and charged the beast, stabbing at it without mercy.

"That'll teach you to snarl at me…take this and take that!" I circled the huge pile, now confident that I had conquered the ugly monster, "Now I can get some work done."

"So, City Boy, where does one begin?" I asked myself, as I folded my arms. "At the top, bottom, and everywhere in between!" I answered back. One thing for sure, I knew this was no one-day project, and not having a lot of barn clean-up experience under my belt didn't help matters either. There were tractor parts, tires and worn out milking equipment everywhere. One and sometimes two of just about everything used on the farm was scattered from one end of the barn to the other. Then, added to the mess, broken bales of hay covered the floor and stacks of wooden crates filled with empty canning jars lined the walls. *I don't need a broom!* I thought. *I need a bulldozer and a dump truck!*

I took a quick walk around the cluttered barn floor sizing up the task before me. "First, I'll get the floor clean down the center of the barn; so I have room to gather all this into piles," I said, announcing my strategy. "After that's done, I'll let my parents figure out what to do with all of this junk." I began by pushing and pulling, then separating and dividing. The wood went into one pile, steel in another, and tires in yet another pile. Little by little, I removed the loose hay and piled it out in front of the barn. With the center of the barn now fairly clean, I began to sweep the floor. Rows and rows of wide, heavy floorboards, which no doubt had been hidden for years, began to appear. As I continued to clear away years of dirt, I noticed several heavy steel hinges attached to the floorboards near the center of the barn. Suddenly, I realized that I was uncovering two very large doors built into the floor. With my curiosity growing moment by moment, I eagerly swept until I could see the complete outline of the two doors.

"They're huge!" I exclaimed. There were no handles on either door, and they looked as if they hadn't been opened in fifty years. I looked around for some kind of pry bar, thinking that with as much junk as there was in this barn, that shouldn't be a problem! I found what looked like a heavy ice pick with a long steel handle hanging on the wall; I grabbed it, ran back to the doors, and jammed it into a crack that ran down the center. Slowly, one of the doors began to lift open. I reached for a small piece of wood with my foot, slid it over and wedged it into the opening. I strained my eyes to look down into the dark hole but couldn't see a thing.

I have to somehow get those doors open and get some light down there, I realized. *As heavy as they are, I need to do it without killing myself.* I just happened to glance up towards the ceiling and noticed several heavy wooden pulleys hanging down directly above the doors. Maybe that's how they did it. If I could hook a rope or chain through a pulley, I'd be able to lift one of these doors. I'd found a heavy rope earlier lying in the clutter and using a long, skinny wooden pole which I had also found, I pushed the rope up through the pulley, then pulled it down and tied one end to the heavy door.

"Now for the defining moment!" I called out. I grabbed the rope, moved back and gave it a pull. The heavy door slowly began to lift open. Now, grabbing the door with my right hand and letting go of the rope, I flung the door open the rest of the way.

As the dust settled, light flooded the hole, revealing what appeared to be some kind of horse drawn wagon. The back of the wagon was filled with picks, shovels, and some miner's lamps. Suddenly, I remembered there was a wagon mentioned in the missing journal page. The excitement of this discovery shot through me like a bolt of electricity. I didn't know what to do. Should I run and tell my mother or just run around in circles?

"Calm down," I told myself, as I paced back and forth like a caged animal.

"Junior, your lunch is ready!" my mother called out from an open kitchen window. I looked at the wagon down in the hole.

"This will have to wait," I said. I closed the barn doors, replacing the heavy fence posts and went up to the house. My mother was standing there waiting for me at the door.

"Why did you close the barn doors?" she asked. My mind frantically searched for an answer. "I don't want anybody to see what I found," I replied.

"So…what did you find?" she asked.

"Just an old wagon," I said, forcing a blank expression onto my face.

"Okay," she said, not giving it a second thought. "I'm going down to Mrs. Zinker's house for a little while. Your lunch is on the table, and I left her phone number if you need me." With that, she brushed past me and hurried down the driveway.

"I'll be here if you need me!" I called out. "Not that I'm going anywhere!" My mother waved without looking back. I hurried into the house, wolfed down my sandwich, gulped my milk, and then went back to the barn as quickly as I could.

"Now, all I need to do is find a ladder," I said, as I reached for the poles leaning against the barn doors. Just then, a dust covered black car pulled up into the driveway. I recognized the two in the front seat. It was Buck Porter and Mayor Bronson.

"Well, well, what have we here," Buck announced, as he got out of the car. He threw a half-burnt cigarette to the ground as he closed the car door. Mayor Bronson got out, adjusted his wrinkled trousers and came and stood next to Buck.

"If you're here to get a new subscription for that excuse for a newspaper, you've come to the wrong place!" I said, as I walked towards them.

Mayor Bronson snickered in his laughing hyena voice. "I told you his parents would read that story, Buck," the Mayor said, as he adjusted his dirty glasses.

"So, my sources were right after all," Buck said, as he looked around. "Thomas Zinker did sell your parents this dump."

"Have you been reading your crystal ball again, Mr. Porter?" I asked, as I nervously glanced back towards the barn. I remembered I'd left the door inside the barn open revealing the wagon; and I knew for sure, I didn't want these two turkeys anywhere near it.

"Look, kid, we know what's going on," Mayor Bronson said, as he spit tobacco juice on the ground. "We weren't born yesterday. We know William Zinker may have hidden the gold here on this farm and we're going to find it."

For a moment, I didn't know what to say. I couldn't just stand by and let them wander around the place. I needed a plan…some way to get rid of them!

"Look, Buck," The Mayor said, pointing to the pile of hay outside the barn doors. "Looks like the kid has been doing some cleaning in the barn. Come on, maybe it's hidden inside."

I stepped in front of them and nervously looked around. That's when the outhouse caught my eye; instantly I knew what to do. I relaxed a bit and let a big smile sweep across my face. "Okay, okay, you two are just too smart for me," I said, as I stared at the two vultures. "I'll tell you what I know first, then, you tell me what you know."

Buck lit up another cigarette and blew smoke up into the air. "You got a deal, kid, but you go first," he said.

"Okay," I said, nodding my head. "I'll go first. My parents have this book about the great Chicago fire in the 1800's," I began. "It says that most rich folks kept their gold and silver hidden in their outhouses, and I was thinking…" I stopped and deliberately turned and stared at the outhouse in the back yard.

In those few moments, I could almost hear little squeaky wheels turning around in Buck's and Mayor Bronson's empty heads. "Mind if we take a look in your outhouse?" Buck asked, trying not to act too interested.

"Not that we believe the gold is in there," the Mayor added. They pushed me out of the way and hurried towards the outhouse.

I went and stood on the porch and watched to see who would be the first one to go inside. I wasn't going to miss this for the world. And just as I suspected, Buck and Mayor Bronson argued who would be first until they realized there were two doors. They patted each other on the back, shook hands, opened the doors, and disappeared inside. I wondered just how long they'd be in there. I began to count out loud, as if it was a game. "One, two, three, four, five, six!"

Suddenly, both doors flew open with Buck and Mayor Bronson tumbling out onto the ground, and just like I'd hoped, hundreds of bees came out after them swarming like a yellow and black cloud. They kicked and rolled on the ground before getting up and running as fast as they could to the car. I slipped behind the screen door as they ran past. It was a real hoot watching them as they tried to get their windows rolled up. When Buck started the engine, I stepped out onto the porch and waved. I laughed as the Mayor climbed all over the seats swatting at several bees flying around inside the car while Buck struggled to get the car turned around. I waved again as they sped off in a cloud of dust.

Feeling quite confident they were not coming back, I went back to the barn to look for a ladder. I had just begun my search when I heard the sound of an engine out in front of the house. I ran to the front of the barn and pulled the doors closed. I peeked through a crack in the door, and to my relief it was only someone passing by on a tractor.

I returned and carefully closed the door in the floor. "No one is going to see my discovery except Ralph and Becky," I said, as I covered the seams in the floor with loose straw. "It's been closed up this long. One more day won't make a difference." I spent the rest of the afternoon cleaning up and straightening the loft until my parents returned home.

My night in the haunted bedroom was pretty much uneventful, considering what had happened the night before. There were no trains to throw me around the room, no bats circling trying to suck my blood, even the cat didn't make an appearance. With all that excitement missing, one would think I'd have gotten a good night's sleep…wrong! With visions of finding the lost Zinker gold dancing in my head all night, it's a wonder I slept at all. When the early morning sunlight began pouring through one of the bedroom windows, I figured it was time to get up. When I rubbed my eyes and took my first deep breath, the irresistible smell of fresh coffee and bacon and eggs, filled my nose.

"Now that's the kind of motivation I like!" I said, sucking in a second deep breath. Needless to say, I jumped out of bed, quickly dressed, and went downstairs.

"Good morning, Mom...you, too, Pop," I said, as I announced my arrival. When I sat down, they stared at me as if I'd been convicted of killing our furry little visitor…the cat that takes care of the bats. "What?" I asked, as I began filling my plate with food.

"Did you have any visitors while your mother and I were gone yesterday?" my father asked.

"Why?" I asked, not giving my encounter with Buck and Mayor Bronson any thought.

My father held up the newspaper. "We have another story about us in the newspaper," he said.

"Look, Pop, I can explain," I said, as I set my plate down on the table. "I was cleaning the barn when I found this trap door in the barn floor. Below the barn floor is this old wagon. Then Buck and Mayor Bronson showed up and started snooping around. They visited the outhouse and then left…but not before deciding to take some of the bees living in the outhouse with them."

My mother busted out laughing while my father just sat there staring at me like a statue. "You're not making one lick of sense, Junior," he said, as he looked down at the article in the paper.

"Read the article again, Michael," my mother suggested. "For the benefit of our delinquent son," she added. When she said delinquent son, she busted out laughing again.

"All right, Dear, but I don't like it," he said, in a stern voice. He began reading out loud.

BUCK PORTER & MAYOR BRONSON HAVE BRUSH WITH DEATH

Saturday afternoon this reporter, Buck Porter, accompanied by our distinguished Mayor, Moose Bronson, made a visit to our newest residents at 604 Pine Street. It was our desire to officially welcome these folks to our humble little town and offer any assistance, as good neighbors should.

Finding Mr. & Mrs. Wolfe not at home, we extended our hand to young Master Wolfe to be applied wherever needed. For some unknown reason, which now is very clear, Mayor Bronson and I were sent by young Mr. Wolfe to look at the outhouse located in the backyard, to which we eagerly complied. Upon entering the outhouse, we found ourselves engulfed by of a large swarm of deadly African bees that no doubt Master Wolfe had imported illegally to our quiet town. Had it not been for the special bee training this reporter had received while in Africa, and the fearless support of my friend, the Mayor, we would not be alive today. Our suspicions of delinquency were confirmed in young Mr. Wolfe by his deliberate attempt to physically harm us. Not since the attack by the Pig-Meister tribe in Africa on my person, had I been in such danger. In my opinion, an apology, written or otherwise, should be forthcoming from the Wolfe family.

After he'd finished the article, my father almost threw the paper across the table.

"Now, Pop," I said, looking at my mother hoping for some support. "Before your blood pressure goes through the roof, let me explain." My father slowly calmed down as I began to relate what had happened. I told my parents about finding a hidden room under the barn floor and the wagon with the old miner's tools, and about Buck and Mayor Bronson showing up and being determined not to leave until they found the Zinker gold. I told them of my idea to trick the two men into searching in the outhouse, knowing inside there was a huge nest of bees. "Pop, I had to do something to get rid of them; or they would have found that wagon," I said, pointing towards the barn.

My father's faced warmed a bit and he chuckled. "Serves those swabs right!" he said. "They're just lucky I wasn't here!"

“Now, now, Dear,” my mother said. “Remember, you work in this town.”

My father looked at my mother with an irritated look on his face and then folded his arms. “You’re the one who said we have to do something,” he said in a scolding voice.

My mother smiled and patted my father on the back. “And we will, Dear,” she said, with this half-smile on her face. “We will.”

The conversation of our unwanted visitors and the discovery of the wagon pretty much ended there. Although I was very much interested in what my mother had in mind when she said, “We will, we will,” we were running late, and it was suggested that we take a look at the wagon and the journal page after church.

CHAPTER 6

LADIES...CHOOSE YOUR WEAPONS!

Our first church visit to Wannabe Bible Church was pretty much uneventful. The pastor, Joseph O'Hara, turned out to be a pretty good guy, even if he did stand up right in front of the whole congregation and say he'd like to be the first man of God to plant the Christian flag on Mars. I guess I shouldn't be surprised...after all, he lives right here in...you guessed it, Wannabe, Michigan. Even though there were a few of those 'who are you' stares from some people, we just figured it was because of those silly stories in the paper.

"In a few weeks, people in this town will have forgotten all about those stories," my father said, on the way home from church. We pulled up into the driveway and before we came to a complete stop, I sprang out of the truck.

"Junior!" my father called out, as he turned off the engine. "Before you disappear into that barn, can we put off looking at your discovery until this afternoon?" I turned and slowly walked back to the truck and leaned in through the open window.

"The Zinker and Harman families are getting together after dinner at the Zinker house for ice cream and cake and we've been invited," my mother said. "And...we've been told there's plenty for you, and your new friends...that is, if you're interested," she added.

"Ice cream, cake and cookies," I said, as I licked my lips. "I'll choose them over split pea soup any time."

My mother looked at me as if she didn't have a clue what I was talking about. "Whatever," she said, shaking her head.

By the time we had dinner, which my mother insisted on cooking in the antique oven, it was past time to go to

Ralph's house. I grabbed the journal page off the refrigerator, put it into an envelope, and stuffed it in my back pocket. "I'm going!" I yelled out, as I went out the door.

"Junior!" my father called out. "Wait and we'll walk with you!" When my mother finally joined my father and me in the driveway, I noticed she was holding two newspapers firmly under her arm.

"What are you going to do with those newspapers?" I asked.

My father looked at me out of the corner of his eye. "Go on, Mae," he said, nudging her. "Why not tell the boy…he's going to find out sooner or later."

"Find out what?" I asked.

"Mrs. Harman, Mrs. Zinker and I are going to do something about that Mr. Porter and his nasty little newspaper!" She held the newspapers up in the air and swung them back and forth as if she were swatting at flies.

"Like what?" I asked, as I looked at my father for his reaction.

"I'm not quite sure…but something," he said, as he let out a chuckle. "I think your mother and her new found friends want to teach Mr. Porter and the Mayor a lesson they'll never forget." My father laughed again and poked my mother in her ribs with his finger.

She quickly brushed his hand aside and punched him in the arm. "You just wait, Michael!" she said, with a determined look on her face. "We'll show you!"

The Zinker's house was the biggest house on our street. With its fancy white pillars and large front porch, it was quite impressive. Becky and Ralph were sitting on the front porch when we arrived, and they motioned for me to join them. Mrs. Zinker met my parents at the door, and I waited for them to go inside before joining Becky and Ralph.

"So, what did your parents think of our church?" Becky asked, as she passed me a small plate of cookies. I smiled at her for remembering my request.

“They didn’t say too much,” I said, passing the plate to Ralph. “But I think they liked it.”

Ralph leaned forward and looked up and down the street, like he was checking for unwanted visitors. “Becky says you have something to show us,” he said, fastening his eyes on me.

I nodded and pulled the envelope with the journal page from my back pocket. “Is this what you’re looking for, Ralph?” I asked, revealing what was inside the envelope.

When Ralph realized it was the missing journal page, his eyes just about popped out of his head. “Where did…how? I can’t believe you found it!” he said, stumbling for words.

“What is it?” Becky asked, as she looked over Ralph’s shoulder.

“It’s from my great-grandfather’s journal. It’s the missing page we’ve been looking for.”

Becky smiled at me. “So this is what you wanted to show me yesterday,” she said. Ralph continued to stare at the page, unable to take his eyes off of it.

“Go ahead, read it,” I urged. I sat back down, and Ralph began to read the journal page out loud.

July 1, 1928. Three days until Wannabe’s Independence Day festival. I’m still waiting for the construction work between the two buildings to be completed. I have found using out-of-town workers has its difficulties as well as its advantages. The purchase of ten new rock picks and shovels this week was unexpected. Eddie has been given the brass key with the family seal which will open the strong box as well as the heavy doors. The wagon, with its strong box, has been prepared to carry the heavy cargo.

The fireworks display at the park, paid for by the Zinker family, was a brilliant idea! This will assure the downtown will be empty during the transfer of goods.

Ralph looked up and stared out across the yard for a moment, as if he was trying to remember something. “I’ve seen a brass key just like the one described here in the journal," he said. Suddenly, he bolted out of his chair and ran into the house.

Becky looked at me in surprise. "Where's he going?" she asked.

"I don't know," I said, shrugging my shoulders. "He's your friend."

After a few moments, Ralph returned, huffing and puffing, as if he'd run a race. "Look what I found in the attic!" he shouted, holding up a tarnished brass key. "This was my great-grandfather's key!" Ralph reached out, grabbed Becky's hand, yanked her out of her chair, and began swinging her around. I joined in the celebration by stomping my feet and clapping my hands as if I were keeping beat to loud music.

"Now that we have the brass key, what do we do with it?" Ralph asked, as he flung Becky towards me. I smiled and put out my arms.

"What if I told you I found something else?" I said, catching Becky. She turned and looked over her shoulder at me.

"Just what did you find, City Boy?" she asked, as she turned and punched me in the arm.

"I found the wagon and the strong box mentioned in the journal page!"

When Ralph and Becky realized I wasn't kidding, they did their crazy little dance again. By this time Ralph was so excited, he just about threw Becky off the porch. "Where is it at?" he asked, hardly able to contain himself.

"I found a hidden room below the barn floor; it's down there!"

Ralph's mother came to the door and pushed the screen door open. "Hey, it sounds like the natives are getting restless," she said. "Maybe I should bring out the cake and ice cream."

"Not now, Mom," Ralph said, heading for the porch steps. "We have to go down to Junior's house to see something." Ralph motioned for us to join him. "We won't be long," he added. Then like jack rabbits, we raced across the yard as fast as we could.

As we double-timed it down to the old Zinker farm, I took the opportunity to tell Becky and Ralph about my unwanted visitors the day before, and how silly they looked with all those angry bees after them.

"My father read Buck's account of what happened out loud at the breakfast table this morning," Ralph said, as he slapped me on the back. "He laughed so hard, he couldn't drink his coffee!"

"My mother was pretty upset about the story," Becky added. "She said they were going to do something about it."

"Who are they?" Ralph asked.

"She's talking about our mothers," I said, pointing to all of us.

When we got to the barn, I pushed the two heavy fence posts aside and opened the doors. As Ralph and Becky kept watch, I swept the straw aside and then motioned for them to join me. Working together, we carefully lifted open one side of the trap doors waiting for the dust to settle.

"There it is!" I announced, pointing down into the hole. "A genuine, honest to goodness wagon!"

Becky reached over and punched me in the arm. "So don't just stand there, City Boy!" she shouted. "Get a ladder!"

"Okay, okay, I'm going," I said, grabbing the same wooden ladder I'd used the day before.

Then, one by one, we went down into the hidden room; it was like going back fifty years in time. Dust covered the wagon and everything in it. Other than the wagon; the room was pretty much empty. After walking around our discovery several times, we turned our attention to the wooden box that was secured with a heavy brass lock. Ralph slowly pulled the brass key out of his pocket and I stared at it as if it was the only key that could get me out of this crazy town.

"This is the moment I've been waiting for," Ralph said, as he slowly aimed the key towards the lock.

Suddenly, like a blast of a shotgun, an unidentified gravely voice called out. “Hey, who’s in here?”

We stared at each other, frozen in our steps… motionless, not knowing what to do. The old floor began to creak as one, maybe more, persons entered the barn.

“Who is that?” I whispered, looking at Ralph and Becky. They shook their heads as the floor creaked again.

“Hey kids, it’s just us,” a friendly voice called out.

“It’s my father,” I said, turning to Ralph and Becky. “He’s going to pay for that.” Mr. Zinker, Mr. Harman and my father leaned over the open hole in the floor, and I grabbed some loose straw and threw it up at them.

“What are you trying to do? Give us a heart attack?” I shouted. My father smiled.

“It was just a little joke…and besides, we just wanted to see this discovery of yours.”

Ralph held up the brass key. “We have the missing journal page and the brass key,” he exclaimed.

“We were just about to try the key in the lock,” I added.

Everyone watched in silence as Ralph slipped the key into the lock. With a short turn to the right, the lock popped open. He carefully removed the lock and slowly opened the box.

“It’s empty!” he shouted, quickly slamming the lid closed.

“What do you mean, it’s empty?” Becky asked, as she reached over and lifted the lid, looking for herself. “You need your eyes checked Ralph” she said, offering him her glasses. “Look!” Becky reached in and pulled out a worn piece of stationary and blew off the dust.

“What is it?” Ralph asked.

“It’s some kind of hand-written note,” she said, holding it up to the light, “but it’s too dark down here to read.”

“Hand it up here Becky,” her father said, bending over. “I’ll read it.” Becky handed it to Ralph, who then handed it to Mr. Harman. He studied the writing for a moment then read it out loud.

Silver and gold stacked wide and deep,
people here are just like sheep.
Making money is my fate,
for my pleasure I'll change its weight.
Below my bust where I do trust,
many a bar that will not rust.
Use the seal, a light and rope;
otherwise you'll have no hope.
William Zinker, Esq.

He handed it over to Mr. Zinker, who studied the riddle for a moment.

"We need to compare that paper with the missing journal page," I said, expecting Ralph to hand it over.

"I don't have it!" he said, holding out his empty hands.

"Me neither," Becky said, looking at me.

"You must have left it back at your house, Ralph!" I shouted, hysterically.

In a sudden panic, we just about killed each other trying to get up out of that hole. Ralph grabbed the riddle out of his father's hand and we raced back to his house. When we arrived back at his front porch, a baseball size rock with a note underneath it had been placed on one of the lawn chairs. Ralph reached for the note, quickly unwrapped it and read it out loud.

If you ever want to see your precious journal page again, give us one-third of the gold and don't show this note to your parents! Don't take too long to consider this offer because we may just be able to figure out for ourselves where the gold is hidden!

Respectfully submitted,
Buck Porter and Mayor Bronson.

"Why those dirty, low-down snakes!" Ralph shouted.

Suddenly I had this uneasy feeling, as if my only hope to escape this little town had just slipped through my fingers. I flopped down into a chair and buried my head in my hands.

"Now what?" Ralph asked as he and Becky joined me.

I turned and looked at him and shrugged my shoulders. "I don't have a clue, but somehow we've got to get that journal page back."

"What do you mean, 'get the journal page back'?" Ralph's father asked, as the three men came walking up the sidewalk.

"Great-grandfather's journal page," Ralph said. He held up the ransom note and waved it in his father's face. He took the note from Ralph and silently read it before handing it over to my father.

"Sorry, Son," his father said. "I know how much you wanted to have that page from Great-Grandfather's journal. I'm sure you'll think of something." My father handed Ralph the ransom note, and the men quietly slipped inside the house.

Becky reached over and grabbed the ransom note out of Ralph's hand. "Aren't you guys forgetting something?" she asked.

Ralph and I looked at Becky, wondering what she was talking about. "What are we forgetting?" I asked.

"We haven't really studied the riddle yet…maybe it can lead us to the gold!"

In our rush to get back to Ralph's house to find the journal page, we had forgotten to take a closer look at the riddle.

Ralph pulled it out of his pocket and handed it to Becky. "Read it out loud," he said.

Becky cleared her throat and began reading.

Silver and gold stacked wide and deep,
people here are just like sheep,
Making money is my fate,
for my pleasure, I'll change its weight.

"Stop right there!" Ralph shouted, as he sprang up out of his chair. "*For my pleasure, I'll change its weight* could mean exchanging paper money for gold!" Ralph then motioned for Becky to continue.

Silver and gold stacked wide and deep.

"That could mean gold and silver is stacked somewhere!" I shouted, taking my turn interrupting Becky.

"Read!" Ralph said, sounding a bit impatient.

Becky gave Ralph a mean stare and started reading again.

Below my bust where I do trust,
many a bar that will not rust.

"Wait," Ralph said, holding his hand up, like a police officer stopping traffic. "*Bars that will not rust* have got to be gold or silver."

"But what does *below my bust where I do trust* mean?" I asked, looking at Becky.

"Come on, Becky," Ralph said, grabbing her by the shoulders. "You've got the school smarts; now think!"

Becky looked up towards the sky. "Think, think," she muttered under her breath.

"Bust could mean to break something. It also means a sculpture or painting of somebody important."

"Are there any statues in or near town?" I asked.

"There's a fountain in the park with a small statue," Becky pointed out.

"Wait a minute," Ralph said, as he jumped up out of his chair. "Remember how the journal page mentioned a tunnel being constructed and how the cargo would be moved into town during the fireworks? The gold has to be somewhere near..."

"Near a statue, a painting or something broken!" Becky shouted, finishing Ralph's words.

"What's broken, Dear?" Becky's mother asked, as she came out of the house and stood on the porch. Before Becky could answer, Mrs. Zinker and my mother came out and joined Mrs. Harman.

"Oh, nothing," Becky said, flopping back down in her chair.

"Nothing but Ralph's dreams," I said, finishing Becky's sentence. I stood up and winked at Becky.

"Mother," I said, in a whiney voice. "They're at it again." I walked over and laid my head on my mother's shoulder. "When we went to the barn to look at the wagon, we left the journal page right here on the porch; and when we came back, it was gone."

"That's the gospel truth, Mrs. Wolfe," Becky added. "Buck and Mayor Bronson came and stole Ralph's most precious earthly possession. Show them the ransom note, Ralph." Ralph handed the note over to my mother who read it before passing it around to the other ladies.

As each one of them silently read the ransom note, I could see the steam building in their faces. The note was handed back to my mother who then gently handed it back to Ralph.

"That does it," she said, in a low, firm voice. "Ladies," she said, turning and facing the other two women. "During war-time, we women always waited for our men to come back home. Now…it's our turn to go to battle!" She put her hand out towards Mrs. Zinker and Mrs. Harman. "For justice," she said.

Mrs. Zinker put her hand on top of my mother's hand. "For freedom," she said.

When Mrs. Harman put her hand on last, she shouted, "For…Ever!"

"Come on, soldiers!" my mother ordered, pointing to the door. "We have things to do!" They all did an about face and marched back into the house.

Becky grabbed me by the neck and gave me a hug. "I sure am glad your mom is here," she said, with a big smile on her face.

"Hey, what about me!" Ralph asked, pulling Becky by the arm.

Becky spun around and punched Ralph in the arm. "I'll give you a punch in the nose…that's what I'll do!" she said, dancing around like a boxer.

"All right, you two, we need to decide what to do next," I said, pretending to send them to their corners.

"We need to do two things," Ralph said, holding up two fingers. "First, we need to make three copies of this riddle so each of us can have one…that way we can study it during this week and try to figure it out."

"What's the second thing we need to do?" Becky asked. Ralph stuffed the ransom note in his pocket.

"We need to get our cake and ice cream before it's all gone. My brain always works better after I've had dessert."

"Now that you mention it, I do, too," I said, rubbing my stomach.

"Me three," Becky added, pushing Ralph and me out of the way. "Last one to get his desert is a smelly plow boy!"

CHAPTER 7

LIFE GETS WEIRD ON THE FARM

The next few days around Wannabe ended up being some of the most boring days of my life. Ralph had to work all week at the hardware store, and Becky had to help her mother prepare for some kind of cookie baking contest. Then, while I waited on them, I was stuck playing old McDonald, who had to clean out a barn.

My father had made it very clear to me the importance of getting the barn cleaned out, saying the rest of our possessions were being shipped to Wannabe sometime early next week. "We just can't pile everything outside," he said. "And, if you keep at it, you should have that chore done in a couple of days."

A chore, he called it. I hate that word, "C-H-O-R-E." Everyone does chores in the country. Clean out the barn, Junior…do your chores, Junior. Slop the hogs, feed the chickens, Junior, and don't forget your chores. Chores, chores, chores! Why can't they just call it something else? In the city they call it…well… something else. One thing for sure, when I get back to the city, I never want to hear that word again! As I thought of the word, 'chore' over and over again and how much I hated it, I had an epiphany.

"Wait a minute," I said, holding a finger up in the air. "Who says that chores have to be started at the crack of dawn? What's keeping me from doing my chores say…in the afternoon? Maybe I'll just sleep in tomorrow until I'm good and ready to get up and do my c-h-o-r-e-s. My parents are always saying young people need their sleep, so why shouldn't I be a good son and listen to them?"

Someone once said that hope springs eternal. Or was it spring's hope is eternal? Or maybe eternal hope has springs? Whatever it was, my hope was that Monday would be the beginning of the end of my having to stay here in this dump of a town. Sure, I liked Ralph, and I hoped he would get his journal back. And Becky…she was fun to be around, and cute, too, but deep down, I wanted to figure out for myself where the gold was hidden and be eternally grateful for being able to get out of here.

But as fate would have it, I was about to be taught a lesson in reality. What's that old saying…man plans and God laughs? Or was it, God laughs every time man plans? Whatever it was, God was about to get a good laugh at me. It was sometime around five in the morning, give or take a few minutes, when I was suddenly jolted from a sound sleep by the most obnoxious sound I'd ever heard. As I lay there, somewhere between the dream world and half awake, trying to get my brain to process what I was hearing, I realized it was an over-zealous, I'm going to drive everybody crazy, rooster. Once that obnoxious bird began squawking, or whatever a rooster does before the sun comes up, it wouldn't stop! If I thought my father would allow me to get his shotgun, or if I could steal one from the neighbor, I would search out that feathery beast and silenced it once and for all. Just one shot God…that's all I ask. Animals making that much noise that early in the morning should be removed from the face of the Earth.

"Don't make me hurt you, rooster!" I shouted, as I pressed my pillow around my ears. No sooner had my threatening words flown out of my mouth when the bird suddenly stopped. I breathed a sigh of relief and relaxed thinking a neighbor had finally given that silly bird what it deserved…to be next Sunday's dinner! I fluffed my pillow and jammed it under my head eager to go back to sleep when a blast of a train whistle sounded off in the distance. Then, as if my pillow had suddenly sprouted wings, it flew across the room hitting the wall.

"Not again", I whined. "Not again!" I could feel my whole body stiffen as I reached down and grabbed onto the bedsprings trying to prepare myself for another roller coaster ride around the room. Then at the sound of a second blast of the train whistle, the bed suddenly came to life. It turned in half-circles and bumped from wall to wall, knocking over the bed stand and everything else in its path.

Why didn't my parents take this room? They were crazy enough to buy this place. Why should I have all the fun? Maybe I'll just move out to the barn. It's probably safer out there. Just as the second blast of the train whistle brought the bed to life, a third blast settled the bed back into its original position. I sat up and pinched myself to see if I was awake. Now wide eyed and breathing like a race horse, the thought of counting my blessings, which wouldn't take too long, or counting my losses, which would take days, or even counting sheep, wouldn't put me back to sleep!

Now…absolutely, totally, and without a doubt awake, I dragged myself out of that death-bed and got dressed in my, 'I'm going to do "chores" the rest of my life' clothes, and went down stairs. When I finally made it to the kitchen, my father was sitting at the table reading our 'favorite' local newspaper.

"Where's mom?" I asked, as I plopped down into the chair across from him. My father tipped the paper down and looked at me.

"You'll know soon enough," he said. He lifted the paper up and began reading again.

"What's going on, Pop?" I asked, as I reached for a box of cereal and a half-gallon bottle of milk.

My father pushed the paper aside and reached for his cup of coffee. "Frankly, I think your mother is crazy," he announced, sounding very matter-of-fact.

"What do you mean 'crazy'?" I asked, studying my father's facial expression.

He raised his eyebrows and chuckled. "You'll see," he said, nodding his head. He grabbed his lunch off the table and went to the door. "Tell your mother I love her and I'll call her from work." He opened the door and then paused for a moment. "Like I said, Junior," he said, smiling at me. "Good luck with your mother. You're going to need it!" Having given me his odd warning, he slipped out the door.

Not having a clue what he was talking about, I dismissed it from my mind and concentrated on my breakfast. I was just about to dig into my cereal when my mother marched into the kitchen, and I do mean literally marched! "Front and center, Private!" she yelled out.

I was so startled by the tone of her voice; my spoon flew out of my hand and bounced across the table. I jumped up and without hesitation stood at attention. My mother stood there dressed in this olive-green, over-starched, baggy army uniform. Her pants appeared to be too long and the shirt too big. She had on an oversized drill sergeant's hat and polished black combat boots, which also appeared to be three sizes too big for her small feet. I bit my lip and tried not to stare.

"Yes, Ma'am," I said. "Front and center!" My mother paced up and down the kitchen floor several times while I stood there not moving a muscle.

"For the next several days, my fellow soldiers and I will be training here at this base," she began. "You are to go about your regular civilian activities unless otherwise informed.... Is that understood?"

I nodded my head without looking at her. "Yes, Ma'am, I understand!"

"Good!" she said. After a few tense moments, a hint of a smile came across her face. "So, what do you think?" she asked, grabbing my shoulders and turning me towards her.

"I think...umm...Dad was right."

My mother's eyebrows lowered. "What did your father say?" she asked.

I cleared my throat and tried to swallow. "He told me to tell you he'd call you from work," I said.

My mother studied my face for a moment then grabbed some papers off the table and walked to the door. "I need to go to the gas station and talk to Mr. Stubbs about a piece of army equipment. If anybody should call, tell him I'll be back in a few minutes." I followed her out onto the porch and watched as she walked down the driveway heading in the direction of the gas station. A car drove past and swerved, just about running off the road.

I just stood there shaking my head. "Now I know what Pop was talking about," I said, as I continued to stare. "She has gone crazy!"

I went back into the house and finished my breakfast then, following my father and my mother's orders, I went back to moving more stuff out of the barn. *These people must have been pack rats,* I thought, as I kicked some loose trash out of my way. I surveyed the growing piles of junk. *They even saved their old, smelly work clothes. Work clothes...work clothes.* I pondered these two simple words... 'work' and 'clothes.'

Suddenly I had this idea. *Hey, if my mother can wear an army uniform, why shouldn't I be able to wear the old farmer's clothes?* I began sorting and sifting, looking for a shirt, pants and overalls. *If my parents want to be farmers,* I decided, as I threw a dirty shirt in the air, *I'll give them a farmer!* After my brief shopping spree, I settled on a worn flannel shirt with, what I assumed was a mixture of horse and chicken manure permanently rubbed into the fabric. Next, I found some disgusting pants and overalls that looked as if they'd been worn five years beyond their usefulness. Then, to complete the new me, I finished off my wardrobe with a slightly used red hanky and a dry-rotted straw hat.

I grabbed up the clothes, went into the barn and made the change to the new me. *When Pop sees me, he'll think both Mom and I have gone crazy and take us back to the city*, I thought, with a sly look on my face. I posed for a moment in front of a broken mirror I'd found in the barn. *Not bad*, I thought, as I grabbed the straw hat off my head and began waving it back and forth. *I sure hope this works because I don't know how long I can put up with the pungent odor from these old clothes*. I threw the hat up in the air and then swatted it with my hand.

"Now, if only I could figure out that silly riddle, then I could find the gold and get out of this flea bag town!" My loud voice echoed through the empty barn scattering a small flock of barn swallows in every direction. I took the riddle out of my pocket and began reading it over and over, as if I were some little kid trying to learn a poem at school. I must have read it fifty times or more before finally stuffing it back into my pocket in frustration. I hated to admit it, but it would be Ralph and Becky, not me who would figure it out. After all, they'd lived here all their lives, and I was, well, just an outsider. I resigned myself to the fact that I'd have to do something I hate…and that would be…waiting!

It was shortly after noon when my mother returned home from her visit to the gas station. To my surprise, she was driving an old army Jeep. "What do you think?" she asked, as she pulled up in front of the barn.

"What's the Jeep for?" I asked, answering her question with a question.

Instead of answering my question, she just stood there staring at me. "What are you up to?" she asked. I responded with a 'I don't know what you're talking about' look on my face. "What do you mean?" I asked.

"Those clothes you're wearing!" she said, almost shouting. "They're discussing!"

"Oh, these clothes?" I asked, turning in a complete circle. "These are my chore clothes." She just rolled her eyes and shook her head.

"So, answer my question," I said, as I pretended to wipe my nose with my new hanky. "What's the Jeep for?"

"For the mission," she responded as she got out and kicked at one of the tires. "Can't win a battle without heavy equipment, you know."

"Is that so?" I asked. She nodded and then turned and made a beeline straight for the house. I wondered just how many people from Wannabe had seen her in that ridiculous baggy army uniform and driving that beat up old Jeep.

I shrugged my shoulders and went back to fulfilling my life's ambition to be a professional barn cleaner. As much practice as I was getting, I was sure I'd be president of my own company in no time at all.

Ever wondered how smart chickens are at five o'clock in the morning? Considering their brains are no bigger than a pea, you'd think they'd be no smarter than dirt. They're so dumb, they stick around the farm and give up all their eggs to the farmer, then overeat, get fat, and finally end up on somebody's dinner plate. Now that's really dumb! But then there's always the exception to the rule. I'm talking about a certain rooster…my worthy opponent. He was not like the rest of those feathery beasts across the street that quietly scratched around for food. Oh, no! His mission in life was to make my life miserable. No doubt he knew me very well because every morning, before the sun came up, he positioned himself, aiming his big beak right towards my window and then, like a blast of a fog horn, which sort of reminded me of Mrs. Harman, out it came.

"Go ahead, rooster, do your duty while you can," I threatened, shaking my finger. "Trust me, there'll come a time when you'll pay for your insolence, and if I have my way, you'll make me a tasty Sunday dinner one of these days."

Wondering why I asked the question of how smart chickens are at five o'clock in the morning? Because when I forced my eyes open, rolled over, and looked at my alarm clock, you guessed it, it was five o'clock in the morning! I wasn't planning on getting up until ten o'clock!

"Stupid bird!" I shouted, as I threw my pillow across the room. "It's still pitch black outside…so much for my plan to sleep late!" I gritted my teeth and listened as the rooster crowed over and over until I couldn't stand it anymore. "One of these days," I groaned, sitting up in bed. "I'm going to teach you a lesson you'll never forget!" Knowing it was futile to try and get back to sleep, I climbed out of bed and got dressed in my chore clothes. I took a deep breath and sucked in the stale aroma of my disgusting outfit.

"Perfect," I said, feeling quite proud of myself. Now confident I'd be totally repulsive to my father, I went down stairs. My hope was that this would be the morning he'd concede to the idea that this country life was affecting my brain, and it would be better for us to move back to the city rather than allow me to slip forever into insanity. I quietly slipped into the kitchen where he was sitting, drinking his coffee and reading the newspaper.

"What is it about that paper that you like so much?" I asked, as I grabbed an empty bowl and sat down.

"I can't get over how this Buck Porter fellow can write such uninteresting hogwash and still stay in business," he commented.

"Is there anything written in there about us washing hogs?" I asked, as I reached for the box of cereal.

"No! And I'd like to keep it that way," he answered, making it sound like an order. He lifted his nose into the air, like he was trying to identify some strange odor and began sniffing the air. "Speaking of hogs, what's that smell?" he asked.

"It's my new perfume," I announced, with a sarcastic voice. "I call it hog wild; I'm told the girls just love it."

My father shook his head. "You keep wearing that perfume and I'll guarantee there will be no girls in your future." I reached for the cereal and the milk.

"Hey, Pop, notice anything new out in the driveway?" I inquired, as I filled my bowl with cereal. My father looked up from the newspaper and stared at me for a moment.

"Are you referring to the Jeep sitting outside?" he asked. "That's your mother's idea."

"So, where's the Captain now?" I asked. "Is she off fighting a war in Borneo?"

"Is that what you're calling her…Captain?" my father asked, in his sarcastic voice.

I nodded my head.

"It was on her orders," I informed him as I looked around to see if my mother, the warrior, was nearby. "So, Pop, what's she up to?" I whispered, leaning in towards him.

He got up from the table and stared out the window at the Jeep in the driveway. "I promised your mother I'd be tight lipped about the whole thing, so you'll have to ask her for yourself." He looked at his watch and mumbled something about somebody being here soon. He grabbed his coffee and walked to the door.

"Who will be here soon?" I asked, looking around the room.

He just smiled and went out the door. "You'll see," he said.

It was only moments after my father had left when three all too familiar ladies, dressed in army uniforms, came busting through the door. "Front and center young man!" my mother ordered. I stood up and faced my mother while the other two ladies moved around behind me. "Ready to go to work, Private?" my mother asked.

"Yes, Ma'am," I snapped. "But I have one question."

"What's that?" my mother asked.

"Are you going to tell me what's going on or am I going to have to wait and read it in Buck Porter's newspaper?"

"It's simple, Junior," Mrs. Zinker said, as she slowly backed away from me. "We're going to get Ralph's journal page back and teach Mr. Porter and Mr. Bronson a lesson, all at the same time. Does that answer your question, young man?"

Before I could say a word, my mother grabbed me by my shoulders, turned me towards the door, and politely told me that I stunk and to get out. "We need this space for some training," she informed, handing me my half-eaten cereal along with my straw hat. With all three women staring at me, I submitted to their request and headed for the door.

"At least I can have some peace and quiet out in the barn!" I shouted back over my shoulder. From a safe distance up in the barn loft, I watched as my mother and her army recruits began working on their master plan…to get Ralph's journal back. They practiced driving the jeep up and down the driveway and communicating with hand signals. They did these crazy exercises where they crawled around on the ground followed by several sprints around the house. I could just imagine what the neighbors were thinking seeing three grown women, all dressed in baggy army uniforms, running around in circles. And what if Buck came by and saw this circus? He'd write another whopper of a story about my family and their negative influence on their innocent little town of Wannabe. "My father's hair is going to turn white when he sees tomorrow's paper," I thought out loud.

By Tuesday evening, just as I planned, I was smelling like what one may describe as rotting garbage...only much worse. When my father returned home from work, it wasn't long before he and my mother came up with this plan to force me to clean up. I was given the choice to get rid of my 'new' clothes, and I use the term 'new' clothes loosely, and to take a shower or, to find a place to sleep in the barn. When a fifteen year old goes up against his parents, guess who wins most of the time? I bowed to my parents' will and took a shower but didn't necessarily get rid of my 'chore' clothes. Hey, I didn't recall ever promising I'd get rid of them forever. Forever is an absolute…I didn't think absolutes applied in this situation.

Wednesday morning: One more day in the life of a prisoner. Five o'clock…rooster wouldn't stop crowing…I wanted to kill him. I was eating the same old, cold cereal…cold and soggy. Embarrassment: My mother and her friends look like clowns. And don't forget…chores, chores, and more chores. Such are the words that described life in Wannabe. I sat up in bed and looked around my room, hoping this would be my last day there. From somewhere outside, my ears detected strange singing or a couple of cats fighting. I went to my bedroom window praying it wasn't my mother and her friends doing their crazy workout again. I watched in horror as half the neighbors on our street lined up to watch my mother and her commando friends standing out in the yard doing their strange exercises as they sang this strange song over and over.

"We are women hear us roar; give us grief, we'll even the score. Up in the morning with our cup of joe, we'll take on the battle to defeat our foes. Sound off, one, two, three, four, let's go!" When they finished singing their battle song, the crowd gave them a rousing ovation. Now, more than ever, I was beginning to wonder if I'd helped in creating a monster. Making those ladies think we were poor defenseless little kids, who somehow needed their help, was probably a big, big mistake. If this went on much longer, I would have forgotten what it's like to have a normal life. And just how much cold cereal can one guy eat before his insides turn to mush? A man has to have a decent meal if he's going to do hard chores. I needed scrambled eggs, bacon and warm toast. But no, I had to eat something that resembled what one fed the farm animals.

"Hey, rooster!" I shouted, looking across the street. "You're looking better as a meal all the time!" I went down to the kitchen and rummaged through the refrigerator, hoping I'd find some real food, when the storm troopers burst through the door. They were huffing and puffing, like they'd just run five miles. They gathered in the corner, like a group of football players, whispering about their strategy to get the journal page back. When I tried to listen, the Captain told me in no uncertain terms I was better off if I didn't know. She then went on to say if I knew what was good for me I'd make myself scarce like the day before. Then to make matters worse, as if I had begged for it, she filled a bowl with cereal and eagerly handed it to me.

Needless to say, I spent another exciting day in my favorite place…the old barn. You know, as strange as it sounds, the barn was beginning to feel like my second home. I had even arranged several bales of hay to look like a couch and chair. I completed my furniture ensemble by adding an old wooden table and lamp. "This is not too bad," I said, feeling quite proud of myself. "Now all I need is a bedroom set."

As I sat on my couch of hay forcing down another bowl of cereal, I wondered if Ralph and Becky had made any sense of the riddle; I was getting desperate. How much longer would this nightmare go on? Should I call Ralph and Becky and tell them I can't wait any longer? This town just wasn't big enough for this barn and me. Either I find that gold soon or…I'd be stuck here and turn into somebody like Wilson or Mr. Stubbs! I'd eat cereal mixed with pea soup and collect toilets the rest of my life.

"Junior!" my mother called out from the porch. "Ralph called and asked you to meet him and Becky at the hardware store in the morning."

I put my hands together and held them up towards heaven. "Thank you, thank you, God!" I shouted. This was the call I'd been praying for. Maybe Ralph had finally figured out a clue that would lead me, I mean us, to the gold. Needless to say, the rest of the day, I must have looked at my watch a thousand times.

CHAPTER 8

A PLAN IN THE WORKS

Thursday: Normally, Thursday is a day just like any other day, except on this day, my life hung in the balance. My hope, my prayer, was that today would bring good news…with Ralph and Becky having figured out where the gold was hidden or, if nothing else, news that my favorite rooster would be part of Sunday's dinner. I rolled out of bed and looked out the window expecting to see my mother and her newfound friends rolling around in the dirt playing army. To my surprise, the old army Jeep was still in the driveway but the yard was deserted.

I recited a new prayer while I got dressed. "Please, please, please, God, let there be real food waiting for me in the kitchen," I begged, as I slipped on my shoes. "Please let there be scrambled eggs," I pleaded, as I went down the stairs. "Please let there be bacon," I whined, as I walked towards the kitchen. My small ray of hope, my crumbling grasp on reality, quickly disappeared when I came through the kitchen door. Rather than finding a delicious home-cooked breakfast waiting for me, a map of what looked like a drawing of downtown Wannabe was spread across the table. My mother had this wooden pointer in her hand and she was aiming it at the train station as if it were significant.

"The cereal is over on the counter," she said, using her pointer. I walked to the counter and stood there staring at the soggy putrid cereal. As I pondered the thought of throwing the bowl of cereal across the room and watch it splatter on the wall, I was suddenly aware that all talking had stopped.

"Okay, what's going on?" I demanded, as I turned and faced the map on the table.

"Ever heard of a bait and switch plan?" my mother asked, as she handed her pointing stick to Mrs. Zinker.

I shook my head. “No,” I answered. “Should I have?”

“It’s simple,” Mrs. Harman said. “We inform Buck Porter and Mayor Bronson that another important journal page has been found. We then set up a meeting and when they try to compare what they have with what we have, we make the switch. Quite simply, they end up with the fake one while we reclaim the real one.”

Mrs. Zinker then stepped in front of Mrs. Harman and pointed her white, flour-covered finger in my face. “Then, to make sure those old goats don’t bother any of us again, we’re going to…”

My mother cleared her throat interrupting Mrs. Harman. “Ladies, ladies!” she said, shaking her head. “We don’t need to burden the boy with the details of our strategy.” My mother walked to the counter and grabbed the bowl of cereal and handed it to me. “Don’t you have something to do, Junior?” she asked, pointing at the barn.

“Yes, Captain,” I said, nodding my head. I walked over to the door. “Oh, just a reminder, Captain,” I said, turning around. “I’m going A.W.O.L. in about an hour. I’m going up town to meet Becky and Ralph.”

“Oh, just a reminder, Junior,” Mrs. Harman said, with a stern voice. “Tell Becky she can’t get involved with this A.W.O.L. thing, she has to be home soon to help me with c-o-o-k-i-e-s!"

“Oh, just a reminder, Junior,” my mother added. “You’re not leaving this property wearing those disgusting clothes!”

Then, as if Mrs. Zinker somehow felt the need to add in her two cents, she cleared her throat to get my attention. “Yes, Mrs. Zinker?” I asked, giving her the green light to tell me what to do.

“Oh, just a reminder, Junior,” she said, completing this ridiculous conversation. “Tell Ralph we’re having steak for dinner.”

I just rolled my eyes and nodded. “I promise I’ll keep Becky from going A.W.O.L. I promise I’ll change my clothes before I go…and Mrs. Zinker, if you have any scraps left from dinner, don't give them to your dog; send them down here to me!"

After forcing half my cereal down and changing my clothes, I headed for Becky's house. As expected, she was waiting for me out on her front porch when I arrived.

"You wouldn't have any bacon and eggs hidden in those over-alls would you?" I asked, pointing to her pockets.

Becky laughed. "What's wrong, City Boy? Aren't you getting fed at home?"

"If you had cold cereal for breakfast, lunch and dinner for several days straight, you'd feel like I feel." I bent over and pretended like I was going to throw up.

"I have some fresh cookies cooling on the kitchen table," Becky said, pointing towards the house. "How many do you want?"

I stood up as if I suddenly felt better. "I'll take at least six!" I said, holding up fingers from both hands. "And don't short me on the chocolate chips!"

Becky went into the house and quickly returned with a handful of warm cookies. I ate every last one as we slowly walked towards town. Becky talked of her mother's odd behavior and how the cookie baking had gotten out of control. I in turn, related the strange event about the neighbors gathering at my house to watch as our mothers exercised and sang. Before we had finished laughing, we were standing in front of the train depot.

"Any sign of Buck and the Mayor?" I asked, as Becky looked up and down Main Street.

"The coast is clear," she said. "Let's run!" We raced across the street and stopped in front of the hardware. Ralph was there waiting for us inside and he quickly opened the door.

"Come on in. The store is empty," he said, motioning with his hand.

"What do you mean 'empty'?" I asked, as I looked around.

"It always is around this time," Ralph said, directing us to the check out-counter.

"So, anybody had any luck with the riddle?" he asked, as he turned to Becky and me.

We took turns shaking our heads.

Ralph turned and began pacing up and down the creaky wooden floor, like he was thinking.

"How about this," I said, holding up my hand to stop Ralph. "Just for argument's sake, let's say we've figured out every part of the riddle except the part that says, *below my bust, where I do trust, many a bar that will not rust*. Had any thoughts on that part?" I leaned against some wooden boxes, which pushed against a pocketknife display on the counter, which in turn, fell to the floor. When I bent over to pick up the mess, I whacked my head on the edge of the counter; this caused me to stumble backward and fall on the floor.

"Junior, are you okay?" Becky asked, as she came and stood over me. I stared up towards the ceiling, momentarily feeling as if I was floating in space. When I finally returned to Earth, my eyes focused on the painting of William Zinker hanging on the wall. Suddenly I remembered Becky's words on Sunday, when she'd said a bust could be a painting of somebody important; I realized I was looking at a bust!

"*Below my bust where I do trust*!" I shouted, pointing up at the painting. Becky looked at Ralph.

"What's he talking about?" she asked, as she reached down and pulled at my arm.

"The painting!" I exclaimed. "It's a bust! *Below my bust, where I do trust*! Ralph, the gold is hidden below your great-grandfather's painting!" I stood up and pointed at the painting again.

"It's been here all the time!" I said. Ralph, suddenly realizing the gold may be hidden right under his feet, jumped up and down and hollered like a farmer calling in his pigs.

"You did it!" Becky said, grabbing me and kissing me on the cheek.

After a few moments of celebration, we calmed down and began to think about what we should do next to locate the gold.

"Junior," Ralph said, pointing at me. "You'll be in charge of transportation. We'll need something to move the cargo."

"Like a wagon with a strong box?" I asked, with a smile on my face. Ralph and Becky laughed.

"Wouldn't a wagon be a little conspicuous?" Ralph asked, folding his arms.

"And we need a horse," Becky chimed in.

"A wagon without a horse does pose a problem," I said.

"Wait a minute!" Becky said, almost jumping up and down. "What if we decorate the wagon for the parade this coming Saturday? We could borrow Mrs. Polk's old mare; she's as gentle as a lamb."

"Okay, Becky," Ralph said, reaching for the pencil perched on his ear. "You're in charge of getting the horse. Junior, you help Becky dig up some decorations."

"What…me?" I asked, putting my hands on my hips. "Where am I going to find decorations?"

"Look in that old barn of yours!" Ralph said. "With so much stuff in there, you shouldn't have any trouble." Ralph pointed to some tools hanging on the wall. "I'll supply the ropes, lanterns, and whatever other tools we need," he said.

Two old farmers came strolling into the hardware and waved at Ralph. "I'll be with you in a minute gentleman!" Ralph called out. "Junior," Ralph said, whispering. "You're going to need heavy rope and some pulleys to get that wagon out of that hole in the barn. I'll bring them by this evening and I'll try to get my father to help us. See if your father can lend a hand."

"May I come?" Becky asked. "I can supervise."

"I wouldn't have it any other way," I said. Knowing that Ralph had to go back to work, Becky and I said our goodbyes and left the store.

Within a few minutes, we were back at Becky's house standing on the front porch. "Bring some cookies when you come," I said, as she opened her front door.

She smiled and said she'd do her best. I waved good-bye and hurried home eager to tell my mother about our discovery. When I arrived home, I noticed it was unusually quiet. Inside the house, I found my mother sitting alone at the kitchen table, studying her map.

"Captain," I said, acknowledging her as I sat down at the table.

She looked up and smiled. "Ready for some hot lunch, private?" she asked.

A smile broke across my face that could have lit up the whole room. "Yes, Ma'am!" I said, almost shouting.

She got up and took some warm meatloaf out of the oven. "How did your meeting go with Ralph and Becky?" she asked, as she began cutting the meatloaf into thick slices.

"You're not going to believe this Mom but we figured out where the gold is hidden!"

"You did?" she asked, with a surprised look on her face.

"Right under William Zinker's painting! It's under the floor of the hardware store!"

"So...tell me how you're going to get to it? Is there some kind of hidden trap door?" she asked. She handed me a warm sandwich on a plate.

"No," I said, shaking my head. "There's a secret tunnel that leads underneath the hardware."

"And just where is this tunnel located?" she asked, as she sat down.

Suddenly, my excitement melted away like a bowl of ice cream on a hot summer day. "I don't know and I don't have a clue," I said, as I put my head down on the table.

My mother got up and went to the refrigerator. "Hey, let's have a cold soda," she said. She opened two bottles and handed one to me.

"We had it all planned out," I said, after taking a quick drink. I told her about our idea of getting the wagon out of the barn and decorating it, and then borrowing a horse and pulling the wagon in the parade. Then later, we'd use the horse and wagon to haul the gold.

My mother looked lost in thought for a moment. "Aside from not knowing where the tunnel is located, you have one, no, two problems," she said, holding up two fingers.

"What two problems?" I asked.

"Well, Buck and Mayor Bronson," she said. Again I put my head back down on the table.

"Don't worry, young man!" my mother announced, her voice turning from soft to firm. "The Captain and her recruits have a plan of their own! It's called bait and switch and then feed them to the dogs!"

My mother stood up and began to pace back and forth across the kitchen floor like an army officer. "Whatever I tell you regarding this plan is strictly off the record," she said, in a guarded voice. "I may have to deny taking part in this plan. Not that I would lie mind you." I nodded, letting her know I understood.

"As we speak, our plan is being implemented," my mother began. "By Saturday evening, Buck and Mayor Bronson should be neutralized."

I looked at her with a surprised look on my face. "You are good, Captain," I said, as I took my soda and held it up. "Here's to success and victory!" I shouted.

She grabbed her soda and bumped it against mine. "To success and victory!" she shouted back.

CHAPTER 9

UNEXPECTED HELP

On Thursday evening, much to my surprise, my mother had prepared a complete hot meal. There was none of that cold cereal or week old leftovers. It was a meal fit for a king. During dinner, a discussion about our plan to get the wagon out of the barn, decorate it, and use it in the parade, pretty much brought my father up to speed. Although he didn't quite believe we were really that close to finding the gold, the thought of using the wagon, if we did find the gold, did make a lot of sense. My mother, knowing my father's resistance to what he called 'making waves in Wannabe,' was not quite willing to spell out her whole plan. She simply stated for the record, she would give assistance to her son, and his friends, wherever needed.

While my parents finished their dinner, I excused myself and went out to the barn. Knowing I wouldn't have much time before Ralph, his father, and Becky arrived, I worked at getting the large trap doors open and tying them back, so they wouldn't accidentally close, smashing us like pancakes. While I was down in the hole, trying to figure out how to get the wagon safely out, the floor began to creak, sending shock waves up and down my spine. My heart was pounding as I stretched to look up out of the hole.

"I hope it's not Buck and Mayor Bronson again," I said, whispering under my breath.

"Anybody home?" a friendly voice called out.

"Wilson!" I blurted out, breathing a sigh of relief. "You just about scared me to death!"

The old man bent over the hole and waved. "I see you found it!" he said, giving me a warm smile.

I looked at him with a surprised look on my face. "You knew about this?" I asked.

He smiled again and nodded. "Sure I did! I helped Tony put it down there."

"Why down in here?" I asked.

"Not quite sure why," he responded. "This here wagon was made special for hauling something heavy. Did I ever tell you about…?" Wilson's voice tailed off, and he paused for a moment, as if he was deep in thought. "I remember when Tony and I were kids," he said, closing his eyes. "We were like brothers, you know. We were always at each other's house or fishing at farmer's pond. When Uncle Sam got this country into WWI, we both decided to join the army on the same day. We had it all planned out…we'd join together, train together, and then go win the war for our county."

"So what happened?" I asked, interrupting him.

Wilson opened his eyes. "It didn't work out that way. When Uncle Sam found out Tony had a bad heart, they kicked him out...simple as that. He stayed home here while I got shipped off to France. When I finally came home to Wannabe, I was a broken man. I couldn't eat… couldn't sleep; the horrible memories of the war were like open sores eating away at my soul."

"So what did you do?" I asked.

Wilson smiled. "It was Tony," he said. "Had it not been for my best friend, I wouldn't even be alive today. Did I ever tell you about Tony and Hazel?" he asked. I smiled and politely said no. As Wilson related the same story he'd told me just a few days before, I thought of what he'd said about Tony being his best friend. He must have been a kind and loving person to care so deeply for his friend. I thought of Ralph and Becky and how they'd treated me since I'd arrived in Wannabe.

"Junior!" Wilson called out. "Are you listening boy?"

I nodded as if I'd heard every word.

"So, anyways," he said, continuing his story. "Tony had to make this special delivery to the train depot for the old man. He asked me to help him, but I had to swear an oath not to tell anybody. It was during the fireworks when no one was in town. We pulled up next to the train depot to a side door; then Tony used some special key to get in. While I stood watch, he unloaded whatever it was and took it into the depot. After that, we brought the wagon back here and hid it in the barn."

"Yes," I said, smiling ear to ear. "It all makes sense! The tunnel must go from the train depot, across to the hardware store! Didn't you say that William Zinker also owned the train depot at one time?"

Wilson nodded his head. "The old man owned it up until the day he died."

"Who owns it now?" I asked.

Wilson held his nose, as if he'd just smelled a skunk. "That Buck Porter fellow," he said.

Ralph and Becky walked into the barn and greeted Wilson. "Is Junior out here?" Ralph asked, surveying the inside of the barn.

Wilson smiled. "Down there," he said, pointing. "Looks like you kids are going to do some work."

"We're going to bring that wagon up out of that hole," Ralph said, as he lifted a heavy rope off his shoulders and flopped it down on the floor.

"Did your father come to help?" I asked, looking up at Ralph.

Ralph shook his head. "No," he said, sounding a bit disappointed. "He had to go to the lumberyard. I'm guessing it had something to do with a late lumber delivery."

"So…how you plannin' to bring that wagon up out of the hole?" Wilson asked, as he studied the pile of rope.

Ralph turned to Wilson. "We're going to try and use ropes and pulleys," he responded.

"It won't work!" Wilson replied, looking up at the ceiling. Before Ralph could question why, Wilson stepped in and took charge. "Junior," he barked, pointing with his finger. "Go around to each corner of the wagon and see if there is a steel ring bolted to the frame." I did as he asked and located four steel rings.

Wilson smiled and nodded. "Good," he said. He reached into his pocket and pulled out an old army knife. "Here, Ralph, cut your rope into four equal pieces and hand them down to Junior; so he can tie one end to each of the rings." Ralph did as Wilson asked, and then tossed the ropes down to me.

The old man patted Ralph on the shoulder. "Good job," he said. "Now, Junior, after you've tied a rope to each ring, hand the other ends of the rope up here." I handed them up to Ralph, who then handed them to Wilson. The three of us watched as he took each separate rope and cleverly tied them together to make one strong knot.

"Now," he said, looking upward. "Is there a ladder up to that loft?"

"Over there," I said, pointing towards the back of the barn.

Wilson handed the rope to Ralph and headed for the ladder. "I'm going to lower a chain with a hook down through the ceiling," he said. "Slip the ropes around the hook and then be prepared to get out of the way!" When Wilson started up the ladder, I climbed up out of the hole. A moment later, a small door opened above our heads causing loose straw to come fluttering down. Wilson peeked through the hole.

"Here it comes!" he called out. When the chain was within reach, Ralph grabbed it and slipped the knot over the hook.

"I don't know how he is going to lift that wagon all by himself," Ralph said, backing away from the hole. "But I'm going to do like he said and get out of the way."

"Me, too," I said, taking several steps back.

"Me three," Becky chimed in.

The chain tightened, and the wagon lifted, gently swaying back and forth. The whole barn seemed to creak and moan as the heavy wagon inched upwards.

Wilson called out through the hole in the ceiling. "When the wagon gets high enough, loosen the trap doors and close them! Then I'll lower it to the floor!" The wagon lifted until Ralph and I were able to close the heavy doors as Wilson directed.

"Okay!" Ralph called out. "You can lower it now!"

The wagon slowly lowered until it rested on the barn floor. We unhooked the ropes and the chain disappeared back up into the ceiling.

Wilson came back down from the loft and stood next to the wagon. "Well, what do you think of that?" he asked, with a proud look on his face.

Before we could answer, he pulled his gold pocket watch out of his pants pocket and held it out at arm's length. "Look at the time," he said, pointing to his watch. "I've got to go." We thanked him for all his help and then he headed out of the barn, waving several times without looking back.

"Do you know how long it would have taken us to get this wagon out of that hole had it not been for Wilson?" Becky asked, turning to Ralph and me.

"Too long," Ralph replied, as he went and sat down on the edge of the back of the wagon.

"Helping us get this wagon wasn't the only thing he did for us," I said, wriggling my eyebrows up and down.

"Wait, don't tell me," Ralph said, copying my facial expressions. "He taught you how to tell stories."

"Much more that that," I said. "I think he told me where the tunnel opening is located." Ralph's mouth fell open and I'm sure it just about hit the floor.

"Where, Junior?" Becky asked, as she grabbed me by the arm.

"The heavy door at the side of the depot," I said. "A tunnel starts there and runs under the street over to the hardware, and the brass key you found opens the door."

"How do you know?" Ralph asked.

"Only one way to find out," I replied.

Ralph jumped up onto the wagon and began singing, "We're in the money, and yes, we're in the money!" While Ralph sang, and believe me it wasn't the best singing I'd ever heard, Becky and I joined in and danced to his silly little tune.

After we had thoroughly tested how loud and obnoxious our voices could get, we decided it would be best to close the barn doors.

"No sense giving Buck and Mayor Bronson an opportunity to see what we've found," I said, pushing on the doors.

"I promised my folks I wouldn't stay long," Ralph said, looking at his watch.

"Me, too," Becky added.

"We'll meet back here tomorrow evening," Ralph said, as he squeezed through one of the halfway opened doors. Becky and I followed Ralph outside, and I finished securing both barn doors.

"Keep an eye on the barn until tomorrow, Junior," Ralph said, as he and Becky started down the driveway. I nodded my head.

"Hey, Ralph," I called out, pretending I didn't hear him. "I'll keep an eye on the barn until tomorrow evening."

Becky looked over her shoulder at me. "You better," she said, "or I'll beat you up!"

The early evening sky had begun to turn from a crisp blue color, into a painter's palette of red, yellow, and purple hues. A pair of robins that had made their nest in a tree in the front yard caught my eye as they fluttered about checking on their young. I looked towards the old house; I could see my father through the kitchen window. He was teasing my mother by grabbing her army hat and putting it on his head. She in turn, chased him around the kitchen table punching him in the arm.

"They certainly look happy," I said, in a soft voice. I surveyed the backyard, looking past the little outhouse and on towards the old wooden bridge. I recalled how, just a few days ago, Becky had pushed me into the water wanting to cool off my temper and although I wouldn't admit it to anybody, I liked Becky from the first day I'd met her. I turned back to see her waving, and I smiled and waved back. Even as I waved, I was beginning to wonder about what would happen in just a few hours. If all went as planned, I was going to be part of the greatest gold discovery in the history of Wannabe. I could end up one of the richest teenagers in the whole state of Michigan and be able to leave here and live somewhere else! The words 'leave and live somewhere else,' reverberated in my head, over and over.

"Wait a minute," I said, as if I were going to argue with myself. "Did you just hear what you said? Is this really what you want, Junior?" I kicked at some loose gravel in the driveway realizing how conflicted I felt. I walked over and stood on the side porch mumbling the same words over and over again.

"Make up your mind! Is this really what you want? Make up your mind!"

"What are you talking to yourself about?" I turned to see my mother standing at the door.

"Oh, nothing," I said, in a discouraged tone of voice.

"They're pretty good kids," my mother said, seeing Ralph and Becky off in the distance. "You're fortunate to have met friends like that." I looked away, knowing what she said was true. "I know that moving here to Wannabe has been hard on you, Junior," she said, putting her arm around me. "So tell me, what can I do to help?"

"Just who am I kidding?" I said, thinking my mother wouldn't understand. "I don't deserve any of it!"

"Deserve what?" my mother asked, with a concerned look on her face.

"The treasure!" I said, turning away from her. "It doesn't belong to me! I thought about getting that gold and using it to get us out of Wannabe and back to the city."

"What are you talking about?" my mother asked, grabbing my shoulders and turning me towards her.

"Ralph's great-grandfather's gold," I said. "Don't you see, Mom? Ralph trusted me to help him find that treasure, and I was planning to get it for myself."

"But you didn't," my mother said, squeezing my arms. "You could have gone looking for that gold days ago and had just as good of a chance of finding it as Ralph and Becky. So, what stopped you?"

"I'm not quite sure," I said, staring at her.

"I'll tell you," she said, as she squeezed my arms again. "You're not like Buck Porter or Moose Bronson. The person I see standing right here in front of me is a warm, honest, and giving person. And you must realize that Ralph and Becky trust you because they also see that same warm, honest, and giving person. So what if you're angry about moving far from your home and starting over in a strange town. Most teenagers would be if they were in your shoes." A slight smile came across my mother's face. "You noticed I used the word 'strange.' I'll admit it; this town is a bit strange." My mother took my hands and held them tight. "Look, Junior," she said, looking me in the eyes. "What you're feeling is normal. It's not easy moving away from the only home you've ever known. I didn't want to let on, but I wasn't so sure your father and I would like living here either. But you know what? So far, we're having the time of our lives!"

I smiled and nodded. "I can see that," I said.

My mother paused for a moment and stared up at the early evening sky, as if she were contemplating what to say next. "If you take some time, Junior, and think about it, you'd realize this is not such a bad place to live."

"So, what do I do now?" I asked, as I leaned over the porch railing.

"You dismiss this nonsense from your mind about betraying your new friends and go out there and have a great time looking for that treasure!" My mother gave me a soft cuff on the back of my head. "Show your friends what you're made of and make your father and me proud." She made a fist and held it up to my chin. "Otherwise, I'll have to beat you up."

I laughed at her threat. "That's what Becky says," I said.

"She's a very nice girl," my mother said, as she turned and grabbed the doorknob. "Now come into the house, Private. There's hot apple pie in the kitchen and your orders are to get in here and have some!" I stood up straight and saluted.

"Yes, ma'am," I said. "Right away, ma'am."

After she went into the house, I stood there for a few moments wondering how my mother had gotten so wise in such a short time.

I turned and leaned over on the porch railing and I could still see Ralph and Becky walking. Becky turned back and waved again and again, and I returned every wave. Becky really had been a friend from the first day we'd met; and even though I'd planned to scare her and send her running home, she accepted me, bad attitude and all. And Ralph didn't know any more about me than Becky did, yet he was willing to confide in me about his life-long dream to find his great-grandfather's treasure. I took a deep breath.

"I just hope I won't let them down," I whispered out loud. "Maybe I've misjudged the people here in Wannabe, thinking them all crazy or up to no good. I guess there are some good people here." Becky waved a third time, and I eagerly responded. It was at that moment, I began to realize the treasure wasn't worth the friendship I'd found in Wannabe. "I won't let you guys down," I whispered again. "I promise, I won't let you down."

CHAPTER 10

LET'S GET THIS DAY STARTED!

Finally…it was Friday! For the first time since we'd moved to Wannabe, I was determined to beat that sneaky rooster at his own game. My plan was to wake up at least an hour before he even made a peep. The thought of recovering the Zinker gold had been so strong on my mind during the night, it was a miracle I'd even gotten an hour of sleep. I was out of bed, dressed and downstairs, even before that molting beast came out of his stall, or whatever he sleeps in. For the next hour, I paced back and forth through the house like a caged animal.

Each time I walked into the kitchen, I stared at the clock hanging on the wall, and wondered why the hands moved so slowly. "I think that silly clock is broken," I whispered. "If it doesn't speed up, I'm going to wear a hole in the floor." I leaned across the counter to tap on the clock and when I did, I knocked the top off the metal coffee pot causing it to bounce off the counter and roll across the kitchen floor. I reached out and grabbed the top and held it in my hand.

Suddenly I had this idea. *What if I made breakfast?* I thought. *My parents would smell the coffee and the food, and then they'd get up.* With that thought in mind, I located the coffee beans first. I knew quite well one couldn't have coffee without coffee beans. Second, I needed to figure out how to grind them. I guess I should have paid closer attention to how one grinds coffee because I didn't have a clue. As I looked around the kitchen, I spotted my father's toolbox in a corner.

"Wait a minute," I declared. "I have an idea." I retrieved a hammer from the toolbox and prepared the beans the old fashion way…by smashing them in a million pieces.

Before long, the coffee was brewing and the scrambled eggs were cooking away. Now…all I needed were two sleepy parents to get out of bed. Ordinarily, I was not this impulsive, but today, I was in a hurry to get this day going. Finally, after what seemed like days, my father walked into the kitchen. He looked at the coffee pot; his coffee cup was sitting next to it, filled to the top.

"That's the blackest coffee I've ever seen," he said, looking down over his glasses at me. I wriggled my eyebrows.

"It's my special country blend," I said. "Go ahead and try it"

Without saying a word, he lifted the cup to his lips and took a small drink. He winced and swallowed hard.

"Kind of strong," he whispered. "What's the occasion?" he inquired, as he went to the refrigerator and grabbed the milk.

"I have a lot to do today and I want to get an early start," I answered. He poured some milk into his coffee, making it turn almost white.

"What kind of stuff?" he asked, as he reached for the honey.

"I've got to come up with some decorations for the parade tomorrow," I said. My father nodded and smiled.

"How about us getting started on those scrambled eggs," he said, as he sat down. "I'm starved." I filled a plate and handed it to him.

"Good morning, men!" my mother said, as she marched into the room. Again, like the past few days, she was dressed in her baggy green uniform. The keys to the Jeep and a whistle were hanging around her neck on a chain.

My father looked at her and snickered. "Going out on a secret mission this morning, Captain?" he asked.

My mother went to the counter and poured herself a cup of coffee. "I'm meeting the troops this morning," she informed us. "We have some last minute arrangements that need to be taken care of in town. And, just to let you know, the ladies and I have decided to drive the Jeep in the parade tomorrow."

My father took a deep breath then rolled his eyes. "I hope you and your lady friends aren't carrying any guns in the parade tomorrow," he said sarcastically. "You may accidentally shoot somebody in the foot."

"Very funny," my mother snapped, as she grabbed an egg. My father slid the milk across the table.

"Here," he said, offering to pour. "You're going to need lots of this in your coffee."

"Thank you," she said, as she sat down. "So, Junior, did you and your friends have any luck getting the wagon out of the barn last evening?" she asked, as she tested the coffee.

"The mission was a success, and the wagon is ready for inspection, Ma'am!" I said. I stuck out my chest, feeling rather proud of our accomplishment.

My mother and father looked at me with a surprised look on their faces. My father set his coffee cup down and leaned forward in his chair. "Are you saying you and your friends...?"

"Yep," I confirmed, interrupting him. "It's out of the hole and we want to use the wagon in the parade."

My father smiled and leaned back in his chair. "Okay, I have a few minutes after breakfast. We'll take a look."

Not wanting to wait for my parents to finish their breakfast, I hurried out to the barn. If Becky was successful in borrowing Mrs. Poke's horse, I'd need to have at least one stall cleaned out. For the first time since coming to Wannabe, I was actually excited about doing my chores.

"Will you look at that!" my father exclaimed, as he and my mother walked into the barn.

"What do you think?" I asked, as I walked over and stood next to the wagon. My parents came and joined me.

"Seems strong enough," my father said, as he kicked one of the wheels. "Just like your coffee."

"How are you going to pull the wagon?" my mother asked.

I pointed in the direction of Becky's house. "Becky is going to borrow Mrs. Poke's old mare," I answered. "She'll bring it down this morning...that is, if you say it's okay." I paused for a moment, hoping for my parents' approval.

"It's okay with me," my mother responded, looking at my father.

"If your mother and her friends can drive that Jeep in the parade, then I guess it's okay for you and your friends to have the wagon in the parade," my father added. He pointed to the stalls at the back of the barn.

"I know, I know," I responded, before he could say another word. "We'll need one of the stalls cleaned out for the horse!" My father said good-bye and left for work. My mother went back into the house, and I went to work doing what I did best…chores! I began the task of empting out the stall.

The animal stalls, like the rest of the barn, had also been completely filled with junk. After removing several bales of hay, I found three old cowboy boots, some straw hats, and several sets of old horse harnesses. I stuck one of the straw hats on my head and looked at myself in a mirror hanging on the wall.

"Yep," I affirmed, nodding. "I sure do look like a country boy."

"Junior!" my mother called from outside the barn. "Mrs. Zinker and Mrs. Harman will be arriving in a few minutes. Until then, I'll be in the house waiting for an important phone call if you need me."

"Hey Mom," I blurted out, calling back to her. "Can you do me a favor?" I hurried to the front of the barn and leaned out the door. "Can you be sure to tell your friends you gave permission to use the wagon in the parade?"

She nodded. "I can do that," she agreed. "So…are you and your friends any closer to figuring out where the secret tunnel is located?" she asked, as she came and peeked inside the barn.

A smile swept across my face. I had forgotten all about what Wilson had said the other evening about the special delivery. "Last night when we got the wagon out of the hole, Wilson was here," I said. "He knew exactly how to do it."

My mother smiled. "I was wondering how you guys got that wagon out so quickly."

"That's not the only thing Wilson did for us," I said, as I walked over to the wagon. "I'm pretty sure he told us where the tunnel is located." I related the story about how Wilson and Tony Zinker made a delivery on the Fourth of July, back in 1929, and how that evening, they went to the depot where Tony opened the side door with a special key. I paused for a moment.

"Does any of this sound familiar?" I asked.

My mother chuckled. "It's just like in the journal page," she answered.

"Right!" I said. "The tunnel entrance must be at the side door of the depot! I'm sure that brass key Ralph found in his attic opens that door!"

My mother turned and waved at Mrs. Zinker and Mrs. Harman who had just started up the driveway. "Make sure you and your friends have everything you need to be safe," she said, as she turned to go meet her lady friends.

"We will," I said. She saluted, turned and went out the door.

By mid-morning I had pretty much finished cleaning out one of the animal stalls so I decided to take a break.

This is going to be neat, driving this wagon tomorrow, I thought, climbing up onto the buckboard. I pretended to be a stagecoach driver riding across a dusty trail in the old Wild West.

"Giddy up!" I called out, pretending I was giving orders to the horse. I swung a pretend stick at the lazy horse. "Come on, get going you old mare!" I shouted.

"Who are you calling an old mare?" Becky snapped. I looked up to see her sitting on a black and white horse.

"Howdy, Ma'am!" I drawled, as I tipped my straw hat. "Didn't expect you until later."

“Whoa, girl,” Becky commanded, as she got down off the horse.

“Your ma talked to my ma and, well, here I am.” She grabbed the reins and led the horse into the barn.

“So, City Boy, where do you want this fine animal?” she asked, looking around.

I pointed towards the back of the barn.

“The hotel suite is back that a way, Ma’am.” Becky tugged on the reins and led the horse into the stall.

“We have a small problem,” Becky said, as she slid by the horse and latched the stall door. “Mrs. Poke didn’t have the right kind of harnesses to hook the horse to a wagon.” When Becky said, ‘harnesses’, I remembered finding some of that stuff when I cleaned out the stall.

“Don’t you worry your pretty head, little lady,” I drawled, standing up and sticking my thumbs into the front of my belt. “I have a pile of that harness stuff right over there.”

Becky pretended to curtsey. “I’d work on it now, but I can’t stay too long,” she said, pointing outside. “My mother is already here, and my orders are to get home.”

“Do you know what they’re planning?” I asked, as I jumped down from the wagon.

Becky shook her head. “No, but I do know my mother is still acting rather strange. She barks out orders, and she’s still wearing those army clothes.”

“Mine, too,” I said, laughing out loud. “They’ve been working on some kind of bait and switch plan.”

Becky wrinkled her nose. “Bait and what?” she asked.

“Bait and switch,” I repeated. “It’s something they cooked up for Buck Porter and Mayor Bronson.”

Becky snickered. “Well, whatever it is, it serves them right.”

“Junior…we’re leaving in a few minutes!” my mother called out from the porch.

I walked to the front of the barn. “Okay, Mom!” I called back. I turned to Becky. “Hey, want a ride home in the Jeep?” I asked.

Her eyes got big and she smiled. "You better believe it, City Boy!" she answered.

"Be right back," I told her. I ran over to the house and busted into the kitchen. Mrs. Zinker and Mrs. Harman were leaning over my mother's shoulder listening while she was talking on the phone. "Can you give Becky a ride?" I asked, blurting out the question.

"Yes, this is Mrs. Wolfe," my mother said, in a low voice. "Yes…we're the same people that bought the old Zinker farm." I waved my hand trying to get my mother's attention.

"Can Becky ride with you in the Jeep?" I asked again, trying to say the words clearly.

She turned to me and held up one finger, as if she was asking me to wait. "Yes…this is Mrs. Wolfe…why am I calling? I found something very interesting in our old house, and, hearing how well traveled you are, I thought I'd show it to you. You want me to describe it? It looks like a page from an old journal. No…I haven't shown it to anybody. Yes, I can meet you tomorrow morning at eight o'clock and no, I promise, I won't forget to bring it…thank you." She hung up the phone and turned and smiled.

"It's all set," she announced. "The bait and switch plan is now in place. Ladies," she stated, tapping her wrist. "Let's synchronize our watches. We don't want to disappoint Mr. Porter." My mother and her friends brushed past me heading out the door.

"What about me?" I asked, following after them. "What am I supposed to do?"

"Keep doing your chores!" They all responded in unison, as they marched out to the Jeep. "That'll keep you out of trouble!"

Becky stood at the entrance of the barn, watching as they took turns climbing into the Jeep.

"Remember," my mother called out, as she started the engine and jammed the shifter into reverse. "Don't tell your father about our plan. It will just get him upset." Becky waved as they turned around and headed down the driveway.

"Sure!" I shouted back. "I'll go back to work on the barn! I love chores! After all, this is what I live for!" My mother waved and the Jeep sped away.

"Sorry about not getting you a ride in the Jeep," I said, putting my hands in the air.

Becky brushed the hair out of her eyes. "Its okay, City Boy," she said, reaching for my hand. "Looks like you need a break. Come on and walk me home."

I smiled at the thought of taking a break. "I'd be happy to, little lady," I drawled, taking her hand. "I'd be happy to walk you home."

Later, when my father returned home from work shortly after six o'clock, I was sitting on the porch drinking a soda.

"How's the clean up work going?" he asked, as he got out of his truck.

"Clean-up is not the word to describe it!" I said, as I set my soda down. "That barn is like a junk yard, antique store, and museum, all rolled up in one! I think I even found stuff in there that belonged to George Washington!"

My father laughed. "You never know." He came and stood next to the porch. "I just saw your mother and her comrades in town," he informed me. "They're all dressed up in their, 'going to war', outfits."

"I know," I half chuckled. "They were all here a while ago."

"So…what do you think about the way your mother has been acting?" my father asked. "You know the army clothes, the Jeep, and strange behavior."

I paused for a moment, remembering my mother's words about not telling my father about her bait and switch plan. "You know how women are, Pop," I said, trying to avoid giving him an answer. "When they start wearing army clothes and trying to act like men, well, you never know what they'll do. So my suggestion is to just stay out of their way."

My father considered my advice for a moment before responding. "I'm not quite sure I know what you mean. But, I think I'll take the advice anyway."

I nodded. "That's a good idea, Pop, a good idea."

Considering all the odd things going on in our lives, that evening around the dinner table was about as normal as it could be. We hardly spoke of the missing gold or my mother's odd behavior. Instead, we talked about my father's work and the Fourth of July festival on Saturday.

My father expressed an interest in going to the chicken barbeque at the park after the parade, which had been a long-standing tradition for the locals in Wannabe. And considering what had been written about us in the *Wannabe Warrior* newspaper, I was rather surprised he was so willing to go. My father went on to say Jonathan, Ralph's father, had said the chicken dinners are some of the best eating around, and he and his family would be there if we would like to join them.

"What time will the chicken dinners be served?" my mother asked, as she poured my father a fresh cup of coffee.

"Jonathon said around noon time."

My mother mentioned that Mrs. Harman would be entering her cookies in a baking contest at the park, then later they would be joining the Zinkers for the evening fireworks and they asked us to join them. When she said we'd be joining them, I just about choked on my iced tea.

"Mom!" I said, staring hard at her. "Aren't you forgetting something?"

My mother looked at me for a moment with a blank expression on her face. "Oh, yes," she whispered, realizing her mistake. "Sorry…I did forget something. Michael, Junior will be with his friends tomorrow evening and it will be just you and me." My father leaned back in his chair, wriggled his mustache and crossed his arms.

Oh no, I thought to myself. I knew that look on his face. That was the, I know something is up, look.

He took a deep breath and held up two fingers. "We've had two stories written about us in the paper since we moved here," he said, wriggling his fingers. "Please don't make it three, Junior."

"Don't worry, Pop," I promised, getting up from the table. "We'll stay out of trouble."

My mother reached over and grabbed my arm. "Wait a moment," she said, as she went into the other room. She returned with a box of red, white, and blue decorations. "Here you go," she said, handing me the box. "You can use these on the wagon."

"Thanks, Mom," I said, giving her a peck on the cheek.

She turned me around and gave me a push towards the door. "Now, get out of here and let your father and I have some peace and quiet."

"Yes, Ma'am," I shouted. "Right away, Ma'am."

Ralph and Becky arrived just as I was opening the barn doors. "Hey, anybody home?" Ralph called out, as they walked up the driveway. I turned and faced them.

"Junior, we came up with this idea," Ralph said, as he hurried past me into the barn. Becky and I followed after him.

"So, what's your idea?" I asked, as I went and sat down on a bale of hay.

"After the parade, instead of bringing the horse and wagon back here, why don't we pull the wagon behind the hardware store in the alley and keep it there until evening? That way, when we're ready, we can grab what we need from the hardware, and then head over to the depot." Ralph folded his arms and waited for my reaction.

"Well," I said, glancing towards the horse in the stall. "Sounds okay to me, but what about the horse?"

Becky looked at me with a puzzled look on her face. "What about the horse?" she asked.

"You know, with the heat and all, will the horse be okay tied up behind the hardware all afternoon?"

Becky thought for a moment. "There's a big shade tree right behind the hardware store. We could tie her up there. And, if we give her plenty of water, I'm sure she'll be okay."

Ralph clapped his hands and stomped his foot on the floor. "Then it's settled!" he shouted. "Tomorrow we go for the gold!"

For the next couple of hours, we worked on getting everything ready for the parade. We sorted through the pile of old harnesses and managed to put together one complete set. Next, we decorated the wagon with silver tinsel and draped blue and white ribbons along the sides. When we finished, we stood back and admired our work.

"What's the word from your mother about the bait and switch plan?" Ralph asked, as he adjusted one of the ribbons.

I jumped up onto the wagon and sat down on the seat. "There's a meeting with Buck and Mayor Bronson tomorrow morning at eight o'clock," I said. "They're going to try to switch a fake journal with the real one."

"Did your mother give you any ideas as to what they were going to do?" Becky asked Ralph.

He shook his head. "No!" he said, his voice sounding quite firm. "I'd probably have to interrogate her before she'd give out any information."

Becky put her hands on her hips. "You should see my mother," she said, rolling her eyes. "She hasn't taken that army uniform off since they started working on that plan. To make matters worse, that army training puts her in the mood to bake cookies." Becky opened the bag she had brought from home and pulled out a handful of cookies. "In the past few days, she's baked enough of these to feed an army! Every corner of our kitchen is full of cookies!"

Ralph lunged for the cookies in Becky's hand knocking them to the floor. "You just leave that problem to me," Ralph said, as he picked up the cookies off the barn floor and stuffed them one by one into his mouth.

"Hey, is anybody thirsty?" It was my mother's voice from outside the barn. She walked in carrying three sodas.

"Hey, Captain, you're just in time," I said, as I jumped down off the wagon.

My mother handed each one of us a cold root beer. "Looks like you're ready for tomorrow," she said, looking the wagon over. "Is there anything I can do to help?"

Ralph struggled to swallow all the cookies he had shoved into his mouth. "Yah," he sputtered, spitting pieces of cookies out of his mouth. "How about keeping Buck and Mayor Bronson out of town tomorrow while we go looking for the gold?"

My mother folded her arms and slowly nodded. "I guess it would be nice to have those two bullies out of the way," she pondered. She held her hands behind her back and began pacing back and forth. "Now," she began, holding one finger up in the air. "If it were up to me, having heard how the Rustlers love to gamble with Buck and Moose, I'd visit those boys and let them know that two certain individuals are itching to take their money in a poker game." She turned, walked to the barn door then spun around and faced us. "I'll bet tomorrow evening would be a perfect time for a poker game, wouldn't you say?" She turned and, without waiting for an answer, went back to the house.

Ralph slowly walked over to a bale of hay and sat down. He looked as if he'd just been told he needed all his teeth pulled; his face was white as a ghost.

"What's the matter, Ralph?" I asked. "You don't look so good."

Becky went and sat next to him. "You don't know what the Rustlers are like, Junior," Becky whispered, putting her hand on Ralph's arm. "I've heard they can chew up pieces of steel with their teeth and spit out nails! Even Sheriff Stanton is afraid of them."

Ralph looked up at me. "Arthur Stubbs," he said in a low voice. "You know…the guy that used to deliver newspapers? Buck talked him into going out there to get a story one time and ended up being gone for days! He hasn't been the same since!"

"Come on, you guys," I said, forcing a nervous smile on my face. "The Rustler boys can't be that bad...can they?"

Becky nodded slowly. "If you guys go out there, you're going to need a secret weapon."

Ralph looked at Becky as if she were crazy. "A what?" he asked.

Becky took the bag of cookies and held it up. "A secret weapon!" she repeated. "Stop by my house on the way out there, and I'll give you a bag full of cookies to take to the Rustlers."

Ralph stood up and took a deep breath. "Considering that I can't think of a better plan, we'll go with the cookie idea," he proclaimed. "But for some reason…" Ralph paused for a moment. "If we're not back by parade time, Becky, you better have an army come and rescue us!"

I laughed and slapped Ralph on the back. "Then it's settled!" I said, as I tried to grab the bag of cookies out of Becky's hands. "Becky can get things started here in the morning until we get back…right, Becky?"

Becky reached out and punched me in the arm. "Just make sure you're back in time for the parade," she warned. "We have to be in line no later than half past nine." Becky stuffed the half empty bag of cookies into my hands. "Here you go, City Boy," she said, walking towards the door. "I've got to go; I promised my parents I'd be home early."

"Wait…I'll walk with you," Ralph said, catching up with her. As they walked down the driveway, I couldn't help but have an uneasy feeling about our meeting with the Rustlers in the morning. After all, I saw the look of terror in Buck's and Mayor Bronson's faces when those guys came into town last Saturday.

"Don't forget, Junior, I'll be over early!" Ralph called out.

When he and Becky had crossed to the other side of the street, Becky cupped her hands around her mouth and called out, "Don't forget to say your prayers…you're going to need it!" I waved, thinking, *that's probably not a bad idea.*

CHAPTER 11

A SCARY PLACE TO VISIT

The old grandfather clock that my father so lovingly coaxed into working, chimed six times as I made my way downstairs. I buttoned up my shirt and quickly tucked it into my pants as I walked into the kitchen.

My mother, who had been up for a while cooking breakfast and taking care of last minute bait and switch details, pointed to a plate full of warm pancakes on the table. "I have a few minutes," she said, sitting down beside me. As I soaked my pancakes with honey, I briefed her on our plans to visit the Rustlers; and she gave me her promise not to tell my father. Then after I'd finished my breakfast, I said good-bye and went and waited for Ralph out in the barn.

Ralph was good to his word, arriving shortly before seven o'clock. He pulled into the driveway in his father's delivery truck.

"How did you get your father to let you borrow this old thing?" I asked, as I ran out to meet him.

Ralph reached across and opened the passenger door. "It was my mother's idea," he said, as he backed out of the driveway. "Somehow she knew about our plan, and she had it all worked out with my father. She also said something about giving us cover...whatever that meant."

"That's interesting," I said, as I tried to roll down the window. "My mother sort of said the same thing."

We drove down our street stopping for a moment at Becky's house to get the cookies. Ralph pulled into the driveway where she was waiting for us

"Here," she said, handing Ralph a large paper bag. "Try not to eat any on the way."

"I promise," Ralph, said, as he set the bag on the seat. Becky stepped back from the truck as Ralph shifted into reverse.

"Where do the Rustlers live?" I asked.

Ralph pointed towards Burnt Street. "We turn left drive into town, then west out of town about a mile. You can't miss it."

"So, what's their place like?" I asked, as I tried a second time to roll the truck window down.

"A prison," Ralph whispered, in a low voice. "They have a long dirt driveway, which is littered on both sides with junk cars. At the end of the driveway, an overgrown mess of tangled picker bushes covers tall block walls that completely surround their house. Some people say they have wild dogs that are trained to kill anyone who enters their property!" I swallowed hard at the thought of having to go to such a place.

As we turned and drove down Main Street, people were busy dressing up the town for the parade. Telephone poles on both sides of the street were decorated with an American flag and every building was draped in red, white, and blue. Old cars and antique farm tractors were pouring into town; people everywhere seemed to be in a festive spirit.

I, on the other hand, felt like we were driving headlong towards our doom. Meeting with two brutes was not exactly my idea of a good time. I thought, *I'd rather deal with Buck Porter and Mayor Bronson than have to deal with the Rustler boys!*

"If in fact they have wild dogs, how are you planning to get past them?" I questioned, as I stared out the window. Ralph pointed to a paper bag on the floor next to my feet. It was about the same size as the one filled with the cookies.

"That bag is full of soup bones," he said.

I lifted both bags and smiled a goofy smile. "Which one goes to the Rustler boys and which one goes to the dogs?"

"Here it is," Ralph said, as he slowed down and turned off the road. He came to a stop and turned off the engine.

"Let me do the talking," he warned, as he fumbled with the paper bags. "They know me."

"So, what are you going to tell them?" I asked.

Ralph stared past me out the window for a moment. "We'll tell them that Buck and Mayor Bronson are itching to have another card game and they've been bragging around town about feeling lucky and they'll be waiting for them in town this evening."

"Isn't that stretching the truth a little?" I asked.

Ralph shook his head. "Are you kidding? You should hear those two talking when they're sitting out in front of the hardware. I'll be telling the Rustlers the gospel truth!" Ralph started the engine, and we slowly drove towards the gate.

Ralph didn't exaggerate when it came to describing their place. Junk cars that looked like they'd been through several wars were lined on either side of the driveway. Overgrown bushes and vines covered dingy white block walls that surrounded their house; it reminded me of an ogre's castle. On the other side of a closed gate, a half dozen dogs ran back and forth, looking as if they couldn't wait to sink their teeth into us.

I looked nervously at Ralph. "What do we do now?" I asked.

"Whatever you do," he warned, almost choking on his words, "don't get out of the truck!"

A scruffy looking old man with white hair suddenly appeared at the gates from behind the solid walls. "What do you want?" he yelled out. Ralph stuck his head out the window and waved.

"Hello, Mr. Rustler. It's me...Ralph Zinker! You know my father. He owns the hardware store."

The old man studied us for a moment then slapped one of the barking dogs telling it to shut up. "So…what do you want?" he asked again.

Ralph cleared his throat. "We'd like to speak to Jesse and Billy for a moment."

The old man's eyes narrowed as he continued to stare. "What about?" he demanded.

"It's about Buck Porter and Mayor Bronson, Sir."

The man turned towards the house. "Jesse…Billy!" he bellowed. "Git yer hides out here...now!"

After a few moments the same two men I'd seen in town a few days ago appeared at the gate. "What is it, Pa?" they asked, as they pushed the rowdy dogs out of the way.

The old man pointed to the truck. "These boys want to talk to you...Something about that no good Buck Porter fellow and the Mayor."

Jesse Rustler grabbed the handle on the rusted steel gate and swung it open. The dogs busted through the opening and quickly surrounded the truck. Ralph rolled his window part way up as I nervously looked on. Jesse and Billy followed the dogs and walked up to Ralph's side of the truck.

"So…what about Buck Porter and Mayor Bronson?" Billy demanded.

Ralph swallowed hard and grabbed the two bags on the seat. "First, I'd like to give you some cookies baked by Mrs. Harman," he said, holding them up.

Jesse reached through the half-open window and grabbed one of the bags from Ralph. He reached into the bag and pulled out a handful of greasy soup bones. "What kind of trick you trying to pull kid?" he shouted. Before Ralph could answer, the dogs went into a frenzy, jumping and biting each other, trying to get to the bones.

Ralph shoved the bag of cookies into Jesse's face. "Sorry!" he quickly apologized. "These are for you…the bones are for your dogs!"

Jesse opened the bag and pulled out a handful of cookies. He handed a couple to his brother, and they shoved them into their mouths. "So, kid, what did you want to tell us?" Billy mumbled, spitting bits of cookie all the way over to my side of the truck.

Ralph watched as several wet pieces of cookie slowly slid down his window. "I thought you'd want to know that

Buck Porter and Mayor Bronson have been bragging all over town about how good they are at playing poker. They said they're feeling lucky, and they'd take you boys on any time."

Jesse and Billy looked at each other and began to laugh uncontrollably. "Hey, Pa," Jesse said, kicking at one of the dogs. "Buck and the Mayor want to play some poker. They say they're feeling lucky." The old man joined in on the laughter, bending over and slapping his knees. Billy stuffed more cookies into his mouth, while handing another one to his brother.

"You tell those two fine, upstanding gentlemen, we'll be looking forward to playing a friendly game of cards this evening at nine o'clock sharp," Jesse said.

He pointed over to his father. "Our Pa there, he wants to be a professional card player. Someday he's going to take us all the way to Las Vegas, where he's going to show us how to win a million dollars."

"Why am I not surprised?" I whispered, as I motioned for Ralph to start the engine. While Billy and Jessie threw the rest of the soup bones to the dogs, Ralph quickly turned the truck around; and we high-tailed it out of there. Now I may be guessing, but I don't think he took his foot off the gas pedal until we were halfway back to town.

Becky was just bringing the horse and wagon out of the barn as we pulled up in the driveway. We jumped out of the truck and ran over to meet her.

"We did it…we did it!" Ralph shouted. He grabbed Becky up and swung her around in the air. "The Rustlers are coming into town this evening!"

"And they're not coming for a tea party!" I added. As Ralph swung Becky past me, she reached out and punched me in the arm.

"Good job, City Boy!" When Ralph set her down, she walked to the wagon and grabbed a yellow envelope and held it up in the air.

"Here you go, Ralph," she said. "This is for you."

He took the envelope and opened it, revealing his great-grandfather's journal page. He looked at Becky and shook his head. "But how?" he asked.

"It is not for you to ask," Becky warned, as she bowed. "Only to accept...or something like that." Becky turned and pointed to the horse and wagon. "While you two were having fun, I fed and watered the horse and hooked up the wagon. There's even extra feed for the horse in the wagon and a bale of hay to sit on." When she pretended to wipe the sweat off of her face, I grabbed her up in my arms.

"Here you go, little lady," I drawled, carrying her over and lifting her up onto the wagon. "You deserve to drive."

She turned and curtsied. "Thank you, kind sir," she said, grabbing the reins. "Well…what are you waiting for?" she asked, motioning for us to hop on. "Time's a wasting!" I jumped up and sat next to her, and Ralph jumped into the back and sat down on the bale of hay. Becky gave a little snap of the reins and the wagon started down the driveway.

"Hey, what's in these bags?" Ralph asked, noticing several large grocery bags in the back of the wagon.

"They're cookies!" Becky answered. "We're going to hand them out during the parade."

Ralph grabbed a couple of cookies out of the bag and handed one to me. "Now this is my kind of parade!" he announced, as he shoved a cookie into his mouth.

Becky tugged on the reins and we turned left at the end of the driveway. "Settle back, boys, and enjoy the ride!" she shouted. She puckered her lips and let out a whistle. "We're on our way to a parade."

CHAPTER 12

A DAY TO REMEMBER

By the time we arrived at the high school, where the parade was to assemble, the town had filled up with hundreds of people.

"I never thought this town could hold so many people at one time!" I yelled out to Ralph, who was stuffing another cookie in his mouth. I marveled as a marching band, all smartly dressed in blue and yellow uniforms, marched past us in perfect formation. Following close behind the marching band, were a dozen young kids with their bicycles decorated in bright red, white, and blue. They were practicing doing figure eights as they headed towards the downtown. Next came three clowns dressed like train boxcar bums dancing and waving at everyone. One of the three clowns reached in her half-torn pocket and threw me a cookie. I recognized the cookie as one of Mrs. Harman's, and when I stood up and waved, she nodded and winked at me.

"Hey!" I shouted, thinking there was something familiar about the clown. She just waved again but kept on walking. I just shrugged my shoulders and stuffed the cookie into my mouth.

"Must be my imagination," I mumbled to myself. As a horse drawn concessions wagon slowly rolled past, the air was suddenly filled with the aroma of buttered popcorn and cotton candy. I licked my lips and looked at Ralph wondering if he wanted popcorn or cotton candy. Ralph was busy stuffing another cookie into his mouth. The marching band, which had passed us only a few moments ago, began playing the song "Yankee Doodle Dandy." I stood up and watched as the band changed its formation and continued to play. The whole town seemed to be alive with excitement, and I found myself being drawn into it as well.

Becky tapped the horse, and we were moving again. A tall man dressed in overalls and wearing a straw hat, waved at us and directed Becky to turn the rig around. She pulled on the reins and spoke something to the horse, and in one smooth turn, we were facing the right direction ready to get into line. I was surprised how easy she made it look; it was as if she had done it a hundred times before.

When we came to a stop, she looked at me and smiled. "What do you think of that, City Boy?" She called out.

I smiled back and nodded. "Wow!" I said, shouting over the crowd. "Not bad for a country girl!"

A car decorated with "Vote for Mayor Moose Bronson," which I recognized as Buck Porter's car, pulled up next to us and came to a stop. The colorful Mayor Moose was sitting in the back seat and, as expected, Buck was in the front seat driving. While the man with the straw hat leaned in through the back window and talked to the Mayor, Buck got out of the car and walked towards our wagon. He stopped for a moment and threw his half burnt cigarette at our horse.

"You kids think you're pretty smart sending those women over to get that journal page," he said, as he reached into his shirt pocket and pulled out another cigarette. "Even though that idiot Bronson let them switch the real journal for a fake, it doesn't matter. We already know where the gold is located." Buck glanced around to see if anyone was listening. "Let me give you brats a piece of advice," he warned, in a snarling voice. "If you're smart, you'll stay out of our way." He lit up his cigarette, and then tried flicking the burning match at Ralph. Instead, it fell between his fingers and down inside his boot. Buck looked down, winced in pain, and quickly limped back to the car.

Ralph jumped up and started to follow after Buck, but I reached out and grabbed him by the arm. "Don't pay any attention to him," I said, as I turned Ralph around. "He's lying…and besides, even if they did know where the gold is, the Rustler boys have other plans for those two!"

Ralph's rock hard stare softened and a smile returned to his face. "I forgot about that," he said. "They'll keep Buck and Mayor Bronson busy for sure."

"Hey, you guys!" Becky shouted out, as she pointed. "Isn't that your mom's Jeep?"

I looked in the direction Becky was pointing. "I recognize the olive green Jeep." I said. "But who…"

As it got closer, I couldn't believe my eyes. It was my father, dressed in his army uniform driving the old Jeep. Ralph's father, who was also dressed in his uniform, was sitting in the seat next to him. They both waved as they slowly drove by. Wilson and Mr. Harman were also in the jeep. Wilson was clean-shaven and dressed in a clean pressed uniform decorated with polished metals. The proud old man waved and saluted, and we stood up, clapped and waved back.

The man with the straw hat walked by and told us to get ready to move. "When I give the signal," he said. "Get into line… and once you start moving, don't stop!" As I stood and looked out over the procession, a girl scout troop, all sharply dressed in matching uniforms, walked on past. There were farmers, dressed in their best overalls, proudly driving their antique tractors. Following them was a hay wagon filled with a group of seniors who were playing lively blue grass music. The man with the straw hat waved and called for us to fall in behind the blue grass folks. Again, as if Becky had handled the horse all her life, she easily moved us right into the middle of the street. Slowly but surely, we were heading towards the downtown and hopefully before the end of the day we'd be bragging to everyone about finding the lost Zinker gold.

As we grew nearer to the large crowds of people standing on either side of the road, Ralph opened the bag of cookies, or what was left of them, and began throwing them in all directions. And although at first glance it seemed he wasn't aiming in any particular direction, it did seem odd that all those cookies were going directly to teenage girls.

Every time Ralph reached into the bag for more cookies, the girls cheered all the more. It kind of reminded me of some great baseball pitcher, throwing strikes while the crowd cheered him on.

As we slowly moved along, I couldn't help but notice just about every country boy in town waving at Becky. Some of them were even whistling at her. I guess I shouldn't be surprised considering she is rather pretty...for a girl. Becky glanced at me every time the boys whistled, no doubt wondering what I thought about the attention she was getting. I smiled and looked away as if it was no big deal. Even if it did bother me, and I'm not saying it did, I wasn't going to let her know.

The parade turned out to be nothing like I'd ever imagined. With so many horses, it had all the makings of a rodeo. With all the food, it was like a picnic. Finally, with so many families, it was like a big family reunion. In spite of my attitude towards this small town, I found myself having a great time.

As the parade moved on towards the center of town, I was actually surprised, if not stunned, to see the place so neat and clean. No crumpled up newspapers were blowing along the sidewalks and no broken beer bottles were scattered along the curbs. Even the weeds growing in the cracks of the sidewalks had been removed. The town looked spotless.

Ralph stood up and tossed out the last of the cookies to a group of small kids and then crumpled up the bag and threw it at me. "We'll turn right here and go to the county park," he announced, pointing in the direction of the lake. "After the Mayor's speech, we'll come back to town and park the wagon."

"The Mayor gives a speech?" I asked, making a funny face.

"Every year it's the same speech," Becky said, with a chuckle. "You've got to hear it."

"A speech made by the village idiot?" I asked, shaking my head. "This I've got to hear and see!"

The park entrance was just outside of town on the east side of Wannabe Lake. Large, perfectly shaped elm trees lined the drive into the park and two old rustic pavilions stood side by side just a stone's throw from the beach. One of the pavilions covered a large stone barbecue pit and the other was lined with picnic tables.

Ralph pointed towards the smoke rising into the air. "See that?" he asked. "That's where the chicken dinners are being cooked." The smoke lifted from the stone pit just about covering the whole park and…it smelled wonderful!

The place was a mass of people with more coming all the time. People everywhere were spreading blankets and setting out picnic baskets. Groups of white haired men gathered in small groups, talking politics or about the weather while dozens of small children splashed about in a fountain in the center of the park. Once inside the park, we pulled off to the side; and Becky jumped down and tied the reins to a tree.

"I think we're just in time to hear the Mayor give his speech," Ralph said, as he jumped off the back of the wagon.

We crossed the road and walked over and stood near a wooden podium where several rows of chairs had been set up for the Mayor and Village Council. Mayor Bronson looked at his pocket watch then stood up and posed as Buck Porter took several pictures. He pulled a wrinkled piece of paper out of his suit pocket, and then waited for the high school band to pass by on its way around the park. He stepped forward, adjusted his dirty glasses and put on his politician smile.

"My fellow citizens!" he began. "Once again, it is a real pleasure to welcome you to another Fourth of July festival here in our great town of Wannabe! Even as I speak, I have been looking forward to our up-and-coming local election, where, if elected, it will be my tenth year as your mayor." He paused for a moment while a few people in the crowd clapped. "As you know," he began again, "I am expecting any day now to receive a call from the powers that be in Washington, begging me to come and serve our great nation on Capital Hill." Again, he waited for the same two or three people to clap.

As I looked around at the people's faces in the crowd, I couldn't tell if they were there out of respect for the Mayor, or if they were just waiting for the chicken dinners to be done.

"As you know," Mayor Bronson continued, pointing his finger in the air, "it has been my life long dream to serve as your Congressman. I am here today to tell you that if I am called…I will answer. If I am elected…I will serve. And if by some odd reason I am not called, nor elected, you'll have the good fortune of having me for four more years."

One of the clowns from the parade who had slipped into the back of the crowd called out the Mayor's name. "Hey, Moose, if you're not elected, we could always use another clown!"

The Mayor's face turned beet red as the crowd roared with laughter. He waved and smiled as if he'd been given a compliment. "Thank you for that kind offer," he said, as he pulled two pieces of paper from his coat pocket. "I…I have been asked to give two announcements. First…see Councilman Bart Pawn if you're interested in signing up for a game of horseshoes." He turned and pointed to a rather large, pudgy man sitting under a nearby tree. "Right over there!" he said. "That's him!"

When Mayor Bronson pointed, the overweight man stood up whacking his head on a low hanging branch. With the gracefulness of a beached whale, he fell to the ground face first and then rolled over on his back. I know it wasn't funny, but he looked like a turtle that had been flipped upside down; he kicked and squirmed but was unable to right himself.

"Should we call the fire department, Mr. Mayor?" someone called out. Again the crowd roared with laughter.

"Okay, okay!" he shouted. "If you're interested in signing up for horseshoes, you know whom to see. Secondly, Mrs. Smith has lost her false teeth during the parade again. If you find them, get them to her right away…she'll need them to eat her chicken dinner."

A small boy ran up to the Mayor and pulled on his coat. He leaned over, and the boy whispered in his ear. "I've just been told that the chicken dinners are ready!" he yelled out. "Thank you and have a great day!" Everybody cheered and then quickly headed for the barbeque pit.

"What do you guys want to do?" Ralph asked, as he breathed in the aroma of barbequed chicken right out of the air. "Get our chicken dinners or take the wagon back to town?"

Becky looked at the long line of people. "By the time we get our chicken dinners, it'll be next week," she said. "I say we get the wagon back into town, and then come back. By then, the lines will be shorter."

Ralph and I looked at each other. "Sounds reasonable to me," I said.

"Me, too," Ralph added.

We slipped through the crowds and made our way back to the wagon. We hoped during all the commotion, no one would pay much attention to us leaving…especially Buck and Mayor Bronson. While Ralph and I stood lookout, Becky slowly turned the rig around; and we headed back to town.

Within a few minutes, we were back at the corner of Main and North Lake streets. Ralph hopped down from the wagon and went ahead, looking up and down Main Street.

"All clear," he announced, waving Becky on. He jumped back onto the wagon, and we crossed over Main and turned left into the alley behind the hardware.

"Do you think anybody followed us?" I asked, looking over my shoulder.

Ralph nervously looked around. "I don't think so," he answered half-heartily. Becky slowed the horse's pace and brought us to a stop under a large shade tree in the alley, near the hardware. I jumped down, grabbed the reins from Becky and tied them to an old hitching post.

Becky pointed to an empty metal pail in the back of the wagon. "Hand me that pail, Ralph," she said. "You guys wait here while I go get some water."

"Yes, Ma'am," he said, handing her the pail. "We'll be right here."

Having this gut feeling that Buck and Mayor Bronson were not far away, I nervously paced up and down waiting for Becky's return. Suddenly, I noticed an odor in the air...It was the unmistakable smell of cigarette smoke. I glanced at Ralph, and by the look on his face, he'd already noticed it, too.

"Buck Porter," he whispered.

No sooner did the name come out of Ralph's mouth when Buck and Mayor Bronson appeared from behind a huge oak tree. "Well, well, what have we here?" Buck squealed, as he and Mayor Bronson walked over to the wagon. Buck sucked on his cigarette one last time and threw it to the ground. "Did you kids think you were going to fool us by sneaking away from the park?" He pulled another cigarette out of his shirt pocket, put it to his lips, and then struck a match on his boot. "We know what you're up to," he said, as he puffed away on his cigarette. "We know about the tunnel. We also know about your stupid little wagon."

As Mayor Bronson circled the wagon, I couldn't help but notice his face and shirt were covered with wet barbeque sauce, like he'd eaten one too many chicken dinners. "Look here, Buck," Mayor Bronson said, as he looked down over his dirty glasses. "It's a strong box, just like the one mentioned in the journal."

Buck smiled, as if he'd just accomplished some great feat. "Now, isn't this a coincidence," he said.

"Okay!" I conceded, as I held my hands up. "You two are just too smart for us." I turned to Ralph. "We have to tell them everything we know."

"What?" Ralph asked, his eyes almost popping out of his head. "Are you crazy?" When Ralph grabbed me by my arm, I leaned in towards him and whispered in his ear. "Just trust me," I encouraged. I turned to Buck and Mayor Bronson.

"We found a secret tunnel under the barn at the old Zinker farm," I began.

Mayor Bronson turned to Buck and spit tobacco juice out of his mouth. "You hear that, Buck," he squealed. "They found a tunnel in the barn! See…didn't I tell you the gold was hidden somewhere on that farm?"

Buck smiled as he flipped a cigarette between his fingers. "Just hold on there, Moose," he cautioned, as he lit up his third cigarette. "I'll tell you what we'll do, kid. You tell us where the tunnel is; and we'll help you find your gold."

Mayor Bronson looked at Buck as if he'd just slapped him in the face. "Their gold?" he protested, almost chocking on the words. He spit out half of his wad of tobacco on the ground and kicked it with his foot. "But, but, but…Buck…I thought!"

Buck turned and gave Mayor Bronson a slap across the head. "Shut up!" he scolded. "You sound like an old boat motor."

Buck turned back to me and smiled. "You tell us where and when and we'll meet you," he said.

Mayor Bronson adjusted his glasses and pointed his barbeque stained finger at Ralph and me. "Right…tell us where and when," he repeated. Buck sucked on his cigarette, waiting for an answer.

"Meet us out in front of your office at nine o'clock tonight," I said, giving Ralph a nervous look.

Buck blew cigarette smoke into the air and nodded his head. Then, he and the Mayor turned and left without saying another word.

After they had gone, Becky stepped out from behind some bushes.

"Did I just hear you tell Buck and Mayor Bronson we're going to meet them this evening in front of the depot?" Becky asked, looking at Ralph.

"Hey, don't look at me!" Ralph said, pointing his finger at me. "That was his idea!"

"Look, you guys," I said. "Can't you see this is perfect? We want Buck and Mayor Bronson to be in town at the same time as the Rustler boys…right?" Ralph and Becky nodded their heads agreeing with my statement. "We already know the Rustler boys will be here…right?" They nodded again. "Well then, why not make sure they're all here at the same time?"

Ralph thought for a moment. "Then we should meet at my house no later then eight o'clock," he suggested. "Just in case we need to go over any last minute plans."

"That's a good idea," Becky added.

"Good…then it's settled," I said, as I put my hands on my hips. "Now let's take care of the horse and get back to the park…I'm starved!"

CHAPTER 13

WANNABE…NOT SO BAD AFTER ALL

Just as Mr. Zinker had promised, the chicken dinners were well worth the wait. When we finally got our food, we ate until we were stuffed. And feeling as fat as those silly clowns looked in the parade, we spent part of the afternoon lying on a blanket under a huge oak tree, waiting for our stomachs to settle. Ralph disappeared momentarily and returned with a chess set, and we battled over several games for the right to brag who was the best at strategy. Becky got corralled into helping with the children's games, and then later she joined up with Ralph and me as we watched Wilson and his friends compete in several games of horseshoes. I was surprised how accurate he was…for a skinny old guy; he made throwing those horseshoes look so easy.

After Wilson thoroughly thrashed his opponents, Ralph and Becky took me on a tour around the park. As we walked, we talked about the parade and of the identity of the three clowns. Ralph and I got a good laugh when Becky revealed to us the clowns were in fact our mothers. When I tried to convince Becky I knew their real identities, she punched me in the arm, saying she didn't believe me and that it was her idea that our mothers should dress up like clowns.

When we finally joined up with our parents, my father told us how he, Mr. Zinker and Mr. Harman agreed at the last minute to drive the Jeep in the parade. He went on to say that Wilson was so honored to be in the parade, he cried. We talked about Mayor Bronson's speech and laughed about Mrs. Smith's missing false teeth.

The man with the straw hat, who had directed us into line at the beginning of the parade, walked past announcing the apple pie eating and watermelon seed-spitting contests. Mr. Zinker stood up and challenged Ralph, claiming he couldn't be beaten. Becky made a similar claim saying nobody could beat her in the watermelon seed-spitting event. Within a few minutes, Ralph was facing his father, and I was facing Becky. Just as Wilson had made throwing horseshoes look easy, Ralph did the same in the pie-eating contest. He won the first place prize for beating his father and everyone else that had joined in on the challenge. And what was the prize for the winner? You guessed it…an apple pie! When the pie was given to Ralph, he promptly, without hesitation, handed it off to the first person who walked by. During the watermelon seed-spitting contest, Becky accidentally, or maybe on purpose, spit a seed in my face and we spent the rest of the contest spitting seeds at each other.

After the games had finished, Ralph, Becky and I took our shoes and socks off and walked up and down the beach. Because of the excitement over the parade, not to mention the activities that followed at the park, I had completely forgotten about my anger over ending up in Wannabe. As I stood on the beach and watched Becky and Ralph splash water on each other, I was beginning to feel for the first time I could possibly…just maybe, accept living here in this strange little town.

"Come on, you guys, it's getting late!" my mother called out, as she began packing up one of several picnic baskets. "We're going soon!"

We grabbed our shoes and socks and slowly walked up the hill. The sun was now low in the sky; I looked at my watch. "Six o'clock," I whispered softly. "The day has gone by so quickly." As Ralph talked to Becky about some girl named Samantha, my mind turned to the adventure that lay before us. Just thinking about the gold gave me goose bumps. It's every kid's dream to search for treasure and yet, I had this uneasy feeling about the whole thing. What if we really did find the gold? Would we be rich and famous? And how would finding the gold change things here in Wannabe? I could just see the newspaper headlines tomorrow. "Local Kids Find Gold…Thousands expected to

Flock to Wannabe to Look for Additional Lost Treasures" and, "Strangers Seen Digging up Local's Back Yards."

It was bad enough having Buck and Mayor Bronson obsessed with finding the gold. What would it be like when this hit the papers? Every gold-digging Tom, Dick, and Harry would be flocking to this town!

With the Jeep now packed and ready to go, we said our goodbyes and headed for home. During that short drive, I decided to push all my uneasy thoughts about the consequences of finding the treasure out of my head. Just knowing how important it was to Ralph that we find that gold, made that decision easier. When we arrived home, I went to my room and got my copy of the riddle we'd found in the strong box. I began to read it over and over trying to memorize every word. I turned on my left side and read the riddle. I turned over on my right and did the same. I read it while on my stomach…and on my back. I even tired reading it backwards.

"All this reading is giving me a headache!" I shouted. I stood up and began to pace back and forth, thinking about what we would do after the Rustlers got rid of Buck and Mayor Bronson.

I held my fingers up in the air, as if I was counting. "First, Ralph can be in charge of the equipment like the ropes and lanterns," I announced out loud. "Second, Becky can bring it over from the hardware in the wagon. And while I'm waiting…I could get the side door at the depot opened with the brass key." I nodded, agreeing with myself.

I went back downstairs and glanced at the clock in the kitchen on my way to the porch.

"Seven thirty!" I shouted. "I still have thirty minutes!" I stood there for a moment wondering where my parents were. Something in the back yard caught my eye, and I turned and saw them sitting on the bridge over the creek. They were staring back at me as if I'd gone crazy. I waved and then went and joined them.

"So, Junior, what's going to happen in thirty minutes?" My father asked, as I came and sat down beside them.

"Ralph, Becky and I are going to meet at Ralph's house," I announced. "Then, we're going to meet Buck and Mayor Bronson at the depot."

My father looked at my mother with a concerned expression on his face. "I know I'm going to regret it for asking," he said. "But…I'm going to ask anyway. Why do you want to meet those two clowns?"

My father turned to my mother, realizing he used the word 'clowns.' "Sorry, Dear...no offence," he offered, with a smile on his face.

She smiled back. "None taken," she replied.

I jumped up and began pacing back and forth on the bridge. "As you know, or don't know, after the parade we took the horse and wagon back into town and parked it behind the hardware," I began. "And while we were there, Buck and Mayor Bronson showed up." I related the conversation we had with Buck and the Mayor and how they said they knew all about the wagon, the strong box, and the secret tunnel. When they demanded we cut them in on the gold, I told them about a secret tunnel under our barn.

My father put his hand up to stop me. "You told them what?" he asked.

I smiled nervously, seeing my father's unfavorable response. "I had to tell them something, Pop!"

My mother touched my father's hand trying to calm him down. "Michael," she whispered, in a soft voice. "Let the boy finish."

I began to pace back and forth again. "Since we knew the Rustler boys were going to be in town at nine o'clock to play poker, we agreed to meet Buck and Mayor Bronson at the train depot around the same time and tell them more about this secret tunnel."

My father stared hard at me. "Okay, so what are you going to do, bring Buck and the Mayor over here?" he asked.

"No!" I stated, firmly. "We have other plans for those two!" I held up three fingers. "One…we meet Buck and the

Mayor outside the depot. Two…the Rustler boys come into town and see Buck and the Mayor. Three…they grab them, drag them off to the bar while we look for the gold!"

My father looked at my mother; she was smiling from ear to ear. His hard look softened and his eyes narrowed. "See what you've done to our son?" my father said, pointing his finger in her face. "You've turned him into a treasure hunter!"

"Me?" My mother blurted out. "He's your son, too!" She reached over and punched him in the arm. When he leaned over to block her second punch, she took advantage of him being off balance and pushed him off the bridge. I think I would have given up some of that gold just to have a camera to capture the look on my father's face. For a moment, my father bobbed silently in the water before finally standing up and facing my mother.

She knelt down; the look of regret was written all over her face. "Oh, I'm so sorry, Dear!" she said. "Let me help you, Michael." She reached out and took his hand and with one quick tug from my father, it was my mother's turn to go flying into the water.

My mother struggled to stand up and then tried to punch my father in the arm. He splashed her in the face, then they begun to wrestle. They were like the children playing at the park earlier that day.

I cheered them on as they exchanged splashes. "Give it to him, Mom…let her have it, Pop!" In a few moments, it was over. "As referee, I have declared no winner of this wrestling match!" I announced, trying to sound like the sports broadcasters on the radio.

My parents climbed up out of the water and sat back down on the bridge. My father took a few deep breaths and wiped the water out of his face. "Well Junior," he said, taking off his water soaked shoes. "Now that I've put your mother in her place, I guess I should admit I would have done the same thing had I been in your place. But…at the same time, I want you to be aware; you're dealing with people that are convinced you are getting between them and their money."

I nodded my head. "I know, Pop, we'll be careful."

My mother pushed her wet hair out of her eyes. "So…what are you waiting for?" she snapped, waving her hand. "Go on, get out of here!" She reached out and gave me a push. "If you need us, we'll be at the park," she added. I turned, and without hesitation, ran all the way to Ralph's house.

CHAPTER 14

PERILOUS DANGERS LIE HEAD

In an instant, or so it seemed, I was standing in front of the Zinker house. Ralph and Becky were sitting on Ralph's front porch waiting for my arrival.

"Hey, what took you so long, Junior?" Ralph called out, as he sprang off the porch and met me halfway down the driveway.

Becky stood on the porch steps and waved. "We were just about to come and get you!" she chimed in.

"You guys ready to do this?" I asked, as I looked at my watch.

"Ready as I'll ever be," Ralph replied. Becky quickly joined us, and we headed towards the depot.

The town appeared to be all-quiet as we crossed over the railroad tracks near the rear of the train station. Except for a dog wandering the street and a few trucks parked in front of the bar, the town was just as we expected…empty.

Ralph put his hand out and motioned for us to stop. He took a few steps forward and looked up and down Main Street. The sun was now low in the sky and long shadows were beginning to slowly creep across the street. The flags that fluttered in the mid-day breeze were limp and still. It reminded me of a ghost town in the old west, abandoned and left to fall into ruin.

"No sign of Buck and Mayor Bronson or the Rustler boys," Ralph said, in a low voice. He motioned for Becky to join him. "Cross the street here and go around the post office to the alley. Wait at the wagon until I come." Ralph turned to me. "Junior, you go around that end of the depot and check out the side door, and then meet me in front." I nodded and slowly walked past him. Becky hurried across the street and disappeared into the dark shadows next to the post office.

When I got to the end of the old stone building, I stopped and looked at the heavy oak door. I could tell from the rusted hinges it hadn't been opened in years, and I wondered if we'd even be able to get it open.

When I walked around to the front of the building, Ralph was pressing his face against the window next to the big doors. "Looks empty," he said, in a low voice.

"So, what do we do now?" I asked, as I looked up and down the street.

Ralph turned and leaned against the two huge oak entrance doors. "We wait," he responded. As I nervously paced up and down, Ralph scanned the empty street; and just as we suspected, it wasn't long before the foul smell of cigarette smoke, Buck's unmistakable signature, began filling the air. When I glanced nervously at Ralph, he nodded his head, as if to say, 'I know, I know…they're here.'

From the shadows at the far end of the depot, a familiar voice broke the eerie silence. "Well, well, look here, Moose. It's our partners, Ralph and his side-kick, Junior." It was Buck Porter's sarcastic voice. Buck and Mayor Bronson stepped out into the light and slowly walked towards us.

"I didn't think you boys would show up," Mayor Bronson said, as he crushed a fat beetle under his shoe.

Buck puffed on his cigarette blowing small rings of smoke into the still air. "Where's your little lady friend?" he asked, looking around.

Ralph pretended not to hear the question. He looked at his watch. "Here's the deal," he said, glancing at his watch a second time. "If you stay out of our way, and we end up finding the gold, we'll give you ten percent."

A broad smile broke out across Buck's face, and he began to laugh; Mayor Bronson joined in. Buck sucked one last time on his cigarette then dropped it at his feet. "Look, kid," he said, as he reached for another cigarette. "We can find that gold with or without you. It's your choice."

I slowly walked around and stood behind our two shady friends. "Look!" I said, in a firm voice. "If that gold is in the barn at the Zinker farm, and I'm not saying it is, that's private property." I stepped on Buck's smoldering cigarette and crushed it into the concrete.

Buck laughed again. "What do you think of that, Moose?" he asked, slapping Mayor Bronson on the back. "The boy is telling us what we can and can't do!"

"Well," the Mayor said, as he paused for a moment. "As an elected official of this here village, I have been appointed as Safety Inspector, Fire Chief, as well as head of a bunch of other departments. Therefore, by the power vested in me, I shall write an order for the complete safety inspection and, if need be, demolition order of a certain barn located on the old Zinker farm!" The Mayor stuck his thumbs into each side of his vest, acting rather proud of himself.

Ralph looked at his watch again. "What are we waiting for, kid?" Buck asked, in a taunting voice. "Is your mommy going to come and save you?" Mayor Bronson busted out laughing and tobacco juice dribbled out of his mouth and onto his shirt.

Ralph's eyes narrowed as he stared at Buck. "We're supposed to meet someone in front of the bar, near the blinking light," he said.

Mayor Bronson tugged on Buck's shirtsleeve. "It's probably that Harmon girl," he said. "They're always together."

Buck slapped the Mayor's hand away. "All right, Moose, I get the picture!" Buck growled. He turned and looked up and down the street. "What do you say we all just mosey down there and wait for her," Buck suggested. He and Mayor Bronson turned and walked towards the bar, and Ralph and I slowly followed behind.

The entrance into the bar looked dark and dingy, like the entrance into a cave. Two swinging doors were propped open with bar stools and cigarette smoke rolled out through the opening. The smoke reminded me of when a wet log is thrown into the fireplace.

Buck leaned in through the doorway and took a deep breath. "Ah, can you smell that fresh air?" he asked, flaring his nostrils. "There's nothing like the smell of a smoky bar on a Saturday night."

Mayor Bronson pushed Ralph and me aside and squeezed in beside Buck. "Bu, bu, bu...Buck," Mayor Bronson said, stuttering as he pointed. "Isn't that?" In a split second, Buck and Mayor Bronson were leaning back on their heels. It was like someone had roped them from behind and given a big yank.

"Well, well…if it isn't our poker buddies coming to look for us," Jesse Rustler said, as he stepped through the doorway and out onto the sidewalk from inside the bar. "Hey, Billy…look who's here! It's your buddy Buck and his friend, Mayor Moose!"

Billy busted through the door holding a beer bottle in each hand. "We had a feeling you two were going to be in town tonight!" he shouted. He handed Buck and Mayor Bronson each a half-empty beer bottle. "And seeing how you've been bragging all over town about feeling lucky, Jesse and I figured we'd let you try your luck on us."

Mayor Bronson adjusted his wire-framed glasses then looked at Buck. "But, but, but, I have to…"

Billy grabbed Mayor Bronson and gave him a bear hug, half squeezing the air out of him. "No need to thank me Moose," he said, almost lifting the man off the ground. "I'm sure you'd do the same for me."

"Sure I would Billy," the Mayor said, while struggling to get loose.

"Save your energy for the poker game, Mayor," Billy said, as he dragged him inside.

"I sure hope you boys brought lots of money," Jesse said with a big smile. He gave Buck a push through the doorway and followed him inside. For a moment, Ralph and I stood there listening as Mayor Bronson whined about not feeling well and Buck telling him over and over to shut his big mouth.

I looked at Ralph; he was beaming from ear to ear. "Hey, you look disappointed, Ralph," I said, slapping him on the back. "You sure you don't want Buck and Mayor Bronson coming with us to find the gold?"

Ralph reached out and punched me in the arm. "Come on, City Boy," he said. "Let's get out of here." We turned and walked back to the depot, feeling confident that Buck and the Mayor were going to be busy for a long while.

"Here," Ralph said, as we came to a stop in front of the depot. He handed me his great-grandfather's brass key.

"You work on getting the side door open while I go get Becky and our supplies from the hardware." Ralph looked around, then crossed the road and disappeared into the shadows.

I went straight to the oak door and, after a quick survey to see if anyone was watching, slipped the heavy key into the lock. I turned it to the right and to my surprise, it worked! I took a deep breath and pulled on the door. As it slowly opened, the rusted hinges squeaked, giving me the creeps. I swung the door all the way open then stepped into the dark room.

It was damp and musty smelling, like the same air had been trapped in there for years. I fumbled around for a light switch and tripped over some clutter on the floor. I tumbled out backward through the doorway and fell to the ground. Before I could right myself, a hand touched my shoulder just about scarring me to death.

"What are you doing, City Boy, trying to wreck the place?" Becky whispered as she bent down to help me up.

"Where's Ralph," I asked, as I brushed myself off. Before she could answer, Ralph appeared in front of the hardware; he quickly crossed the street and joined us.

"I knew it," he said, trying to look past me into the dark room. "I knew this was the entrance to the tunnel."

Ralph tossed Becky and me a flashlight. "You guys hold the flashlights. I'll carry the ropes." When he motioned for us to follow him, I reached out and grabbed him by the arm.

"Wait Ralph," I warned, pointing inside. "There's no tunnel. It's storage for a gardener's tools."

Ralph turned and stared at me as if I'd just punched him in the stomach. He threw the ropes on the ground and grabbed the flashlight out of my hand. "Let me see," he said. He flipped a small switch on the flashlight, and light flooded the small room. Becky and I looked over Ralph's shoulder as he poked his head inside the doorway. The small closet had a dirty floor and broken clay flowerpots were piled in every corner. An assortment of worn out hand tools dangled, like strange shaped ice sickles, from every wall.

"I don't understand it!" he shouted, as he kicked the heavy oak door in frustration. "Where's the stairway to the tunnel?"

A thundering boom sounded over the lake drawing our attention away from the small storage room. "What was that?" I asked, looking in the direction of the park.

"That sound means the fireworks will begin soon," Becky said, as she pointed.

"It means we have less than two hours before this town fills up with people," Ralph added. Ralph kicked at an old clay pot then brought his foot down hard on the old floor. The force of his heel sent half the floorboards crashing down into a dark hole below. Surprised, Ralph stumbled, and almost fell; Becky screamed and grabbed his arm.

"I'm all right, I'm all right!" He shouted, as he backed away from the weak floor. Ralph dropped to his knees and reached in and pulled several more boards loose. He lifted them up and set them out of the way.

"Give me your flashlight," he said, holding his hand out. Becky handed over her flashlight, and he directed the light down into the hole. "Just as I suspected," he said, aiming the light beam in several different directions. "There's a stone stairway down there…I'm sure this is the tunnel my great-grandfather built.

“Get the rope, Junior,” he said, as he pulled one last floorboard loose. I grabbed the rope and handed it to him. “Junior, you go first. Then I’ll follow,” he said. “Becky, you come last.” Ralph moved out of the way and watched as I crawled down through the hole in the floor.

“What about the wagon?” I asked, as I stopped and looked back at Ralph.

“What about it?” he asked.

“What if we need it?”

“We’ll come back and get it if, I mean when, we need it,” he said. I slipped the rest of the way down through the hole and waited for Ralph and Becky. Ralph dropped down through the hole, then turned and grabbed Becky’s hand as she came down. I leaned against the stone wall; it felt wet and slimy. We waited momentarily for our eyes to adjust to the darkness before making our way slowly down the stairway. The warm, musty air at the upper entrance of the stairway began to get cooler with each downward step we took. Drops of water fell from the stone walls making every step slippery.

“How much farther?” Becky asked, as she pulled spider webs out of her hair.

“I don’t know,” Ralph said, as he stopped and waited for her to catch up.

Suddenly Becky froze like a statue. Her flashlight dropped out of her hand, and it bounced across one of the stone steps. “What was that?” she asked, her voice sounding a bit unsettled.

“What was what?” I asked, as I stopped and turned around. Becky pointed. “I heard something at the top of the stairs.”

Ralph picked up her flashlight and turned it off. “Becky, did you close the door up there?” Ralph asked.

Becky put her hand on her forehead. “Oh, no!” she said, shaking her head. “I forgot!”

“Junior, turn your flashlight off,” Ralph said, whispering in a low voice. We stood there motionless for a moment as we listened. I put my hand on my chest; my heart was pounding so hard, I was sure whoever it was at the top of the stairway could hear me.

"Well, well, what have we here?" We stared at each in horror; it was Buck's voice at the top of the stairway.

"Look Buck!" Mayor Bronson blurted out. "Those brats led us right to the secret tunnel!"

Buck let out a laugh and his voice echoed down the stairway. "So…there's a tunnel under the Zinker barn, hey?" he said in a sarcastic voice. "We're not falling for that one! Do you hear me?"

"That's right," Mayor Bronson added, "and we never said we wanted to play poker with the Rustler boys either!"

"What are we going to do, Ralph?" Becky asked.

"We wait and listen," Ralph whispered back.

"Come on, Moose, get down there and find those kids!" Buck ordered.

"But, but, Buck," Mayor Bronson, said, protesting in a whining voice. "It's, it's dark down there."

"So, go get us a light!" Buck shouted.

"But I don't have a light," Mayor Bronson whimpered. "Maybe Mr. Zinker would come and open the hardware store so we could get a flashlight."

"You're an idiot, Moose!" Buck yelled out. "Did you hear what you just said? Why do I waste my time asking you to do the simplest task? If I want something done, I have to do it myself!" Buck grabbed an old clay flowerpot and tossed it down the stairway. "I know you brats can hear me down there! I promise you this...we'll be back!" The sound of their voices faded as they walked away arguing about flashlights and avoiding the Rustlers. After a few moments, all we could hear were water drops dripping from the rock walls.

Becky turned her flashlight back on. "What do we do now?" she asked.

Ralph pondered the question for a moment. "We have a choice," he said, as he looked at his watch. "We go on together and hope that those two don't come back, or one of us goes back and makes sure they can't follow us by locking that door."

I reached in my pocket and pulled out the brass key. "I'll go back and then catch up with you," I said.

"Good," Ralph said, giving me a push. "Hopefully, you can buy us some time."

I retraced my steps, back to the entrance where I peeked up through the wood floor. I looked for any signs that Buck and Mayor Bronson may still be nearby. As mad as they were, I didn't want to meet up with those two. I waited for a few minutes then reached for the door and pulled it closed. I put the key in and locked it as fast as I could.

"There…that will teach you guys to fool with us!" I said, stuffing the key back into my pocket.

No sooner had these words come out of my mouth than I heard Mayor Bronson's voice from the other side of the door. "Buck, the door is locked!" he shouted, tugging on the doorknob.

"So, get it open, you idiot!" Buck ordered.

I quickly slipped down out of sight and hurried back down the slippery steps. "We got company!" I announced, as I caught up with Ralph and Becky.

"Doesn't matter," Ralph said in a discouraged voice.

"What are you talking about?" I asked, giving Ralph a hard stare. He and Becky stepped aside revealing two large iron gates blocking the entrance to the tunnel. Becky pointed to a board hanging over the iron gates. It had something written on it and she read it out loud.

Those who come unprepared shall not prevail upon these gates.

"What does that mean?" I asked, as I grabbed hold of the gates and shook them.

"It means..." Ralph took a deep breath. "It means…this is as far as we go."

"What about the brass key?" I asked, as I pulled it out of my pocket.

"Not going to work," Ralph said. He pointed to a large, flat iron bar that was fixed across both gates on the opposite side. "That bar has to be lifted from the other side to get the gates opened," he said.

I turned my flashlight on. "What did the riddle say?" I asked, as I studied the iron gates.

"Use the seal, a light and rope, otherwise you'll have no hope," Becky said, finishing the rest of the riddle.

"The seal is the key, right?" I asked, looking at Ralph and Becky for a little help.

"The light is...well, a light for the dark," Becky added.

"But what is the rope for?" Ralph asked.

I studied the locked gates again and noticed a hole above the gates in the stone wall. "To get us past the locked gates!" I shouted. "Look up there…can you see that hole in the wall? We put the rope through that hole, feed it down on the other side, then pull it back through and tie it in a loop."

Ralph's faced brightened. "Then, we hook the loop on the one end of the bar and lift it!" he said, excitedly. Ralph quickly uncoiled the rope and fed it through the hole in the wall. Becky reached through the bars and grabbed the rope. "Now, tie the rope into a loop and slip it over the end of the bar," he said. Becky did as Ralph directed and tied a slipknot and hooked it on the end of the bar. Ralph gave a heave ho and pulled the rope tight.

"The bar is stuck," he said, as he pulled his hardest. "Come on, you guys…help me," he said, as he tried pulling again. Becky and I grabbed on, and we all pulled together. And as many times as we pulled, the bar was stuck fast and refused to budge.

"What do we do now?" Becky asked, as she pushed her hair out of her face.

"Oh, kiddies, daddy is home!" It was none other than Buck Porter's sarcastic voice.

"And don't forget your Uncle Moose!" Mayor Bronson chimed in. "We're here to help you find your treasure!"

Buck laughed and Mayor Bronson joined in. "We got a big crow bar and forced the door open!" Buck called out, his voice sounding so close. "So ready or not, here we come."

"I haven't come this far to give up," Ralph said, as he pulled again on the rope. "Come on, we can do this!" Becky and I grabbed on and together we gave one more tug. With a loud scrapping sound, the bar began to slowly lift. Becky leaned on the gate and the hinges squealed, as it swung open. "Come on!" Ralph shouted, as he grabbed the iron bar and held it up. We could hear Buck and Mayor Bronson as they struggled to get themselves down through the old wooden floor. Becky wrestled with the knot, trying to get it untied while I kept an eye on the stairway. I was convinced that Buck and Mayor Bronson were going to be on us in just a few seconds.

"Sounds like they're almost here," Ralph said, as he struggled to hold up the heavy iron bar.

"Come on, Becky, come on!" I urged, trying to hurry her.

"I can't, I can't get the knot out!" she cried out.

Ralph's feet began to slip on the stone floor making him almost drop the iron bar. "Hurry up, you guys, and get through the gates!" he said. "I can't hold this bar any longer!"

"Turn your flashlight on, you idiot, so I can see where I'm going!" Buck shouted, scolding the Mayor. He turned sideways trying to squeeze through the wood floor beams while Mayor Bronson tried to help by pulling on one of his boots. Finally, Buck broke free landing on the wet floor with a thud. Mayor Bronson helped him off the floor and tried brushing him off.

"Will you stop that!" Buck demanded, as he pushed Mayor Bronson away. "We're wasting valuable time!"

Becky dropped the rope, and we hurried past Ralph; he let the heavy bar go, and it came down with a loud crash, locking both gates back in place.

Mayor Bronson stopped in his tracks and Buck ran into the back of him. "What was that Buck?" he asked, as he turned and grabbed Buck's arm.

Buck shook him loose. "Let go of me, you big baby!" he shouted. "Do you want to get that gold or not?" Buck stared hard at his friend until he nodded his head. "All right then. Let's get down there," Buck said, giving him a push.

Ralph finally worked the knot out of the rope and started pulling it through the hole in the stone wall as fast as he could. Becky and I watched nervously as he pulled the last of the rope through just as Buck and Mayor Bronson approached the gates.

"Come on, let's get out of here," Ralph whispered. "We don't want them to see us with this rope." He threw the rope over to me and headed farther into the tunnel. Without saying a word, Becky and I quietly followed after him.

Making our way just beyond the gates, the tunnel made a sharp turn to the right. It looked like who ever had dug the tunnel, had run into an old well from years past. It must have been easier to go around then break through. It was a perfect place to get out of sight, so we slipped around the corner and turned our flashlights off. It wasn't a moment too soon. We looked back and there were Buck and Mayor Bronson standing at the gates.

"Buck," Mayor Bronson said, as he pointed. "These gates are locked by an iron bar."

Buck grabbed hold of the heavy gates and shook them. "How did those brats get past these gates?" he asked, as he shook the gates a second time. "Well…don't just stand there, Moose, look around! Maybe there's a secret passage somewhere!"

Ralph motioned to us and we quietly backed away. "Becky," Ralph said, whispering, "just turn your flashlight on; we've got to keep moving." We went around the old brick well and continued moving deeper down into the tunnel. Ralph stopped suddenly.

"Look, a small ray of light," he said, pointing up ahead. He ran down several more steps beyond the range of the one flashlight.

"Ralph!" Becky called out. "You're getting too far ahead of us." No sooner had she given this warning than there came a thunderous crashing sound, as if the whole tunnel were collapsing in on them.

"Ralph!" Becky screamed, as she ran towards the horrible sound.

I dropped the rope and ran after her. When I caught up with Becky, she was kneeling down at the edge of a large hole in the tunnel floor; it looked like some sort of old mining shaft. "I think Ralph may have walked across some weak boards and fell through," she said, as her voice began to quiver. I bent down and directed my flashlight down into the abyss. A cloud of dust streamed up out of the dark hole making the flashlight useless.

"Ralph, can you hear me?" I called out. He didn't answer.

Becky grabbed my arm and started to cry. "Junior, what are we going to do?" she asked.

I looked around; my mind was going a million miles an hour. I didn't know what to do. I knew we couldn't go back because Becky and I couldn't lift that heavy bar across the gates. If anybody was going to help Ralph, it was going to be us. I turned to Becky and took hold of her hands. "Becky," I said, trying to keep my voice calm. "Look at me. This is what I want you to do." I squeezed her hands and looked into her eyes. "Keep calling to Ralph while I see if I can find a large rock. Maybe I can tie the rope off and climb down the shaft."

Becky whimpered and wiped the tears from her eyes. "Okay, but please hurry," she said. While she called out Ralph's name, I went and got the rope. Fortunately, not far from the hole, I found a good sized bolder and secured the rope. I pulled the rope tight and back stepped towards the shaft.

"Junior!" Becky shouted. "Ralph's okay…I can see him now!"

I leaned over the edge of the shaft and aimed my flashlight down into the hole. Ralph had fallen about ten feet down to some sort of wooden floor. He was half covered with debris from the rotted floor that had given away causing him to fall. He appeared to be scraped and bruised but otherwise, okay.

"Ralph!" I called out. "What are you trying to do, give us a heart attack?"

He laughed and then winced in pain. He pulled his left arm close and cradled it with his right hand. "I think my left arm is broken," he said, as he tried to hold it up.

I shook my head. "Now why did you have to go and do that?" I asked, sarcastically.

"I thought we needed a little more excitement," he said, forcing a smile on his face.

Becky reached out and punched me in the arm. "You two going to talk all night, or are we going to figure a way to get him up out of there?"

"Junior!" Ralph called out. "There's a wooden ladder down here that goes down to another wooden floor below me. Use the rope to get down here. Then pull the ladder up to this level, and we'll use it get me out of here."

I set my flashlight down and tossed the rope down. "I'm way ahead of you, Ralph," I said. I tested the rope, making sure I didn't pull the large rock in on us. Then, I lowered myself down into the shaft.

"The ladder's over there," Ralph said, as he pointed with his foot. I reach down, pulled it up and leaned it against the wall.

"Seems sturdy enough," I said, as I looked it over.

"It's going to have to do," Ralph said, as he stepped on the first rung. "I don't think I could get out of this hole without it." Ralph struggled up the ladder while I helped steady him from below. When within reach, Becky grabbed onto him and helped pull him out the rest of the way.

Ralph slumped down onto the wet floor of the tunnel and leaned back against the stone wall. "Sorry about this, guys," he said, as he tried to hold his arm still. "I should have been more careful."

Becky lifted Ralph's shirtsleeve and looked at his arm. "You're going to need a doctor, Ralph," Becky said, as she gently covered his arm back up.

"Oh, boy," he said, as he rolled his eyes. "I get to go see Doc. Forester."

"Who's Doc. Forester?" I asked.

"Doc. Forester lives here in town," Becky said. "He's older than dirt and he…"

"Don't tell me," I said, interrupting her. "He wants to be the first man to fly around the world in a balloon, or some other crazy thing like that." Becky laughed.

"He wants to go to France and learn to be a famous painter," Ralph said. "Every time I see him, he has a doctor's bag in one hand and a paintbrush in the other."

I shook my head. "Considering some of the people I've met in this town, why should I be surprised?"

Ralph groaned in pain as he struggled to get up. "We've got to keep going," he said. "We've got to find that gold. Then get me to Doc. Forester." I glanced at Becky; I could see the concern on her face.

"This time…I go first," I said, stepping in front of Ralph.

One by one, we edged our way past the open hole on an uneven, narrow path along side the tunnel wall. We moved slowly and deliberately, keeping in mind other dangers that might be hidden up ahead. The tunnel made another small turn then ended at a heavy wood door. Ralph ran to the door and tried to pull it open.

"It's locked!" he said, turning around and leaning against the door. I remembered the brass key in my pocket.

"Let's try the key," I said, as I slipped it into the lock. With a quick turn to the right, just like the lock on the door at the depot, it opened. I pulled the door open, revealing the entrance to a dark, cluttered room.

"This is it!" Ralph shouted, as he charged inside. Becky and I followed after him. The room was like a dark tomb that had been sealed up for years. Thick dust covered stacks of dry, rotted wooden boxes and spider webs, like small fishing nets, hung everywhere from the ceiling.

"Do you think the gold is in one of these boxes?" I asked, as I surveyed the room with my flashlight.

"I don't know," Ralph, said, as he tapped on one of the boxes with his foot.

"Hey, I found something!" Becky said, excitedly. Ralph raced over and helped Becky pull a canvas tarp off an old chest. It was a rather large black trunk, with tarnished brass trim and leather handles on both ends. The initials W.J.Z. were barely visible on a worn brass plate.

Ralph put his hand on the trunk. "This is it!" he said, almost shouting. "It's my great-grandfather's chest!" He struggled and lifted the latch and opened it up. What we'd expected was a trunk full of bright, shiny gold coins. Instead, the trunk was full of old books, maps and an assortment of cooking utensils.

Ralph slammed the trunk closed then winced in pain again. "I don't understand," he said, holding his arm close to his chest. "I thought it would be right here!"

Becky put her hand on Ralph's shoulder. "Maybe it's somewhere else and not down here," she suggested. "We can come back another time and look for the gold."

In spite of Ralph's pain, he refused to give up looking for the gold. As Becky and I watched, Ralph searched through the stacks of boxes, hoping to find the treasure.

Suddenly Ralph became excited. "Hey, you guys, I think I may have found it!" he said, as he knelt down and uncovered a small metal box. We joined Ralph as he brushed off the dust.

"It looks about the right size," I said, as I tried to move it, "and it's heavy, too!"

Ralph's pain appeared to be getting worse. His face was now covered in sweat, and he looked flushed. I glanced at Becky. I could tell we were thinking the same thing.

"Ralph," I said, as I put my hand on his shoulder. "You've found the gold; now we have to leave."

Ralph looked at me with a surprised look on his face. "What do you mean leave?" he asked. When he reached down and tried to move the metal box, I grabbed his arm.

"Ralph," I said, in a firm voice. "We need to get you to Doc. Forester. The gold is not that important. We can always come back for it later." I could see the disappointment in Ralph's eyes as he stared at the metal box. Becky looked at me then turned to Ralph.

"Ralph," she said, "look at me." Becky's voice was calm and reassuring. "Junior and I care about you, not about the gold. It doesn't matter if we find it tonight or next year. It doesn't even matter to me if we ever find the gold!"

"I wouldn't go that far," Ralph said, giving Becky a slight smile.

Becky returned the smile. "What matters is that all of us are safe and are friends forever."

Ralph slowly looked around the room. "So close and yet, so far," he said, as he wiped sweat off his face. "Okay, you guys, let's get out of here."

"Ralph, did your father ever mention a secret passage from the hardware down to this room?" I asked, as I studied the contour of the dark walls.

Ralph shook his head. "No, not that I ever remember," he said.

I directed my flashlight to the other side of the room. "Look, there's a wooden ladder over there that appears to go up through the ceiling. I just wondered...." My voice dropped off hoping Ralph would pick up on my thought.

"Is there another way out?" Ralph asked. He stared at the ladder for a moment. "I guess there's only one way to find out. Let's go see."

We pushed some boxes out of the way and made our way over to the ladder. One by one, we began to climb...Becky went first; Ralph and I followed. With his injured arm swollen, Ralph struggled but made it to the top.

“What is this place?” Becky asked, as she surveyed the tiny room with her flashlight.

“I think we’re near the storage room in the hardware store,” Ralph said, as he looked around.

“Everybody…look for a way out,” I said, as I began to tap on the walls. We pushed, pulled, kicked and banged on every wall but we couldn’t find any secret panel or hidden door.

“Why don’t we just kick a hole in the wall?” Becky shouted. She folded her arms and leaned against one of the walls causing it to spin like a merry-go-round. She fell through the opening and out onto the storage room floor. Ralph and I laughed as I helped her up. Ralph studied the secret opening.

“I never knew this was here!” he said, as he tried to figure out how it worked. I looked at my watch.

“It’s after ten o’clock,” I said, touching Ralph on the arm. “Doc. Forester may be back from the fireworks by now.” I jammed a rake handle into the secret opening to keep the door from closing before going out the back door of the hardware. We stopped for a moment, checked on the horse and wagon, and then made our way out to Main Street. While I walked with Ralph, Becky ran on ahead to let the Doctor know we were coming. Within a few minutes, she returned and said he wasn’t there but would be home soon and we were welcome to come in and wait.

“Becky, stay with Ralph,” I said, as we walked up Doc. Forester’s driveway. “I have something important to do.” I turned to leave, then stopped and turned around. “Don’t worry about the horse. I’ll take care of it.” Becky smiled and waved.

“Be careful, Junior,” she said.

“I will,” I affirmed, waving back. “I’ll see you guys tomorrow at church.” Becky waved again and followed Ralph inside. As I hurried away, I knew I had a lot to do and little time to do it.

CHAPTER 15

LOST TREASURE REVEALED

It was early Sunday morning; I rolled over in bed and looked at my clock.

"It's uh…something o'clock," I whispered, as I tried to focus my blurry eyes.

"Junior…Junior!" I could hear my mother's voice from somewhere down stairs. "It's time to get up!"

"Ever heard of Sunday being the day of rest?" I yelled. The old grandfather clock began to chime, and I found myself counting. "One, two, three…seven. Seven o'clock," I said, rolling over to the other side of the bed. Then, as if I needed one more thing to annoy me, the phone began to ring. I sat up in bed and rubbed the sleep out of my eyes.

"Hey!" I yelled out. "Will someone answer the phone?" I could hear my mother answer, and I strained my ears to listen. All I could hear were bits and pieces of this one-sided conversation about Ralph and something about his broken arm. When she was finished, she came to the bottom of the stairway.

"Junior!" she called out, "Breakfast is ready." The familiar smell of fresh brewed coffee, an aroma I've come to love in the morning, filled the house. It made me hungry…it always made me hungry. I stumbled out of bed and went downstairs.

My father was in his usual place, like a permanent fixture, sitting at the kitchen table having his coffee. He looked up and watched me as I sat down. My mother came in holding her coffee cup and sat down beside me. She started tapping her fingers on the table, while she and my father just stared at me. My mother had this silly smile on her face, as if she expected something to happen at any moment.

"Okay, I give up," I said, looking at them. "What's going on?"

"I think your mother wants to hear about what happened last night," my father said.

"We both do," my mother added, "and don't leave anything out." I looked at them and smiled.

"You want to know if we found the gold…right?" I asked.

My mother nodded. "Yes!" she said, emphasizing the word.

"I can't tell you," I said.

My father gave me this browbeating look. "What do you mean you can't tell us?" he asked.

"I don't know yet," I said.

My father leaned back in his chair. "All right, Dear," he said, holding his hands up. "It's your turn."

My mother got up and returned with one small pancake, smothered with honey and one strawberry, on the side. She set the plate down in front of me. "One pancake for one answer," she said, with a, 'I'll show you,' smile on her face. "I'll give another pancake for the details."

I looked at the small pancake and then rolled my eyes. "Not this game again," I said, sarcastically. I picked up my fork. "Okay, you asked for it. We met with Buck and Mayor Bronson…the Rustler boys showed up…Becky left the door open, and I locked it." I stuck my fork into the strawberry and put it into my mouth. "We got past a steel gate…Ralph fell into a hole…he hurt his arm, and we searched for the gold." I cut the small pancake into four pieces and stuffed half of it into my mouth.

"I dropped Ralph and Becky off at Doc. Forester's house…I met the Rustler boys again…I went to find Arthur Stubbs and brought the horse and wagon home and went to bed." I took a deep breath, and then stuffed the rest of the pancake into my mouth.

My father looked at my mother while taking a sip of his coffee. "How come I have this feeling the boy is leaving out some minor details?" my father asked.

"I told you it wouldn't make sense," I said, as I held up my plate for more.

"So, when are we going to get the whole story?" my mother asked.

"After church," I said.

"Why after church?" she asked, as she dropped two more warm pancakes on my plate.

"Look, Mom," I said, as I picked up my fork. "I know you don't understand, but you'll have to trust me. I want you to make arrangements for all of us to meet at the Zinker's house after church. Then you'll find out about the lost Zinker gold."

My mother slid a second plate full of pancakes in front of me. "Okay," she said, shaking her head. "But if they ask me for any details, I'm going to blame you for keeping us all in the dark."

When we arrived at church, Ralph and Becky were waiting for me near the front doors. "What do you think of this?" Ralph asked, holding up a white plaster cast covering his broken arm.

"Nice," I said, reaching out and touching it with my hand.

Becky reached out and punched me in the arm. "Where did you go last night?" she asked, in a low voice.

"I had some things to do," I whispered back.

"What's this about a meeting at my house after church?" Ralph asked, as he looked around to see if anybody was listening.

"It was my idea," I said. "After I left you guys last night, I took care of some things." The church bells began to ring, and everyone standing outside the doors began to file inside.

"I'll explain everything when we get to your house," I said, as I slapped Ralph on the back. He winced in pain and before I could say I was sorry, Becky punched me in the arm for hurting Ralph.

After church, when everyone had arrived at Ralph's house, I directed them all to sit down on the large front porch. And like an experienced lawyer working on an important trial, I began to relate to them everything that had happened the night before.

"As you know, last evening, during the fireworks, Ralph, Becky and I went looking for the lost Zinker gold," I began. "Because of clues that had been uncovered, we knew the location of the secret tunnel entrance. From there, Ralph used his head, or should I say his foot, to figure out how to get into the tunnel. It sounded simple enough, except for two small problems: Buck Porter and Mayor Bronson. Even with our almost perfect strategy, they somehow managed to follow us into the tunnel. And again, if it hadn't been for Ralph's quick thinking, we'd still be down there trying to avoid Buck and Mayor Bronson. But, enough said about Buck and the Mayor. I'll get back to them later.

After Ralph fell and got hurt, we made our way to the hidden room under the hardware where we looked for the gold. Becky and I were concerned over Ralph's injury and we decided to find a way out. Upon finding a secret passage up into the hardware, we got Ralph over to Doc. Forester as quickly as we could." I paused and took a deep breath.

"Becky," I said, looking directly at her. "When I told you I'd see you tomorrow, I was heading over to the bar to find the Rustler boys. They were just coming out as I arrived. They said they were coming to look for Buck and Mayor Bronson who had gone for more money. I took them down to the depot and, wouldn't you know it, here came Buck and Mayor Bronson around the corner. You should have seen their faces when they saw the Rustlers. Jesse and Billy were so mad they threw Buck and Mayor Bronson into their dump truck and drove out of town. On their way out, I could hear Billy and Jesse yelling something about Buck and Mayor Bronson needing a visit out at the farm for a few days. After that, I ran over to the gas station hoping to find Arthur Stubbs. I remembered my pop saying he used to deliver newspapers. You said that, too...right, Ralph?"

Ralph nodded. "Well, I figured with Buck Porter away, it couldn't hurt to have somebody else write an article. We sat down and I told Arthur the whole story, and he promised he'd put it in the Sunday paper. There is one more thing you should know about Arthur, not only can he write, but lifting all of those toilets has made him strong as an ox."

A young boy, carrying newspapers on his bicycle, rode up the driveway and handed me a newspaper. "Special delivery for Junior Wolfe!" he announced.

"Thank you," I said, giving the boy a quarter. "You're just in time." I turned and handed the paper to my father.

"Pop, will you do the honors of reading the front page story?" I asked, handing him the newspaper.

My father looked at me and then unfolded the paper. He looked at the article for a moment then began to read out loud.

THE LOST ZINKER GOLD, THE MYSTERY SOLVED

By: Arthur Stubbs

After years of speculation over the existence of the lost Zinker gold hidden somewhere here in Wannabe, the mystery has finally been solved. During the evening of the Fourth of July, 1959, three teens; Ralph Zinker, Becky Harmon, and Junior Wolfe, armed with clues accumulated over the past weeks and months, uncovered a secret tunnel that supposedly had been built by William Zinker sometime back in the 1920's. The tunnel location, according to Ralph, would not be revealed because of safety reasons and no doubt would be sealed up forever. Quoting an unnamed source, this writer got this statement.

"The tunnel is full of all sorts of dangers," the informed source said. "Anyone not trained in safe tunnel exploration, could be seriously hurt."

With a supply of rope, flashlights and determination, these three young explorers made their way down into the depths of an uncharted tunnel. They fought their way past locked steel gates, winding, slippery steps, and unmarked open shafts. If it hadn't been for their sturdy rope and the quick action of Junior Wolfe and Becky Harmon working together, Ralph, who had fallen down into a deep hole and broke his arm, may have never survived.

The tunnel, which led to an abandoned room under the hardware store, revealed no lost treasure. Although there were some items found like old tools, worn books, stacks of wooden boxes, old maps and cooking utensils, nothing of any great value was uncovered.

"I suspect this will finally put an end to people looking for the lost Zinker gold," Junior Wolfe said, when asked to give a statement. He went on to say that he wanted to thank Becky Harmon for taking such good care of Ralph while waiting for Doc. Forester to return from the fireworks.

My father folded the paper and handed it to Ralph's father.

"Now, for the rest of my surprise," I said, as I pointed to the street. Again, with almost perfect timing, the old mare and wagon, driven by Arthur Stubbs, pulled into the driveway. Everyone stood up and leaned on the railing as he came up the driveway then stopped in front of the porch.

"After Arthur and I finished with the newspaper story, he offered to go back to the hardware store," I said, pointing to the back of the wagon. "He helped me bring up the small metal box Ralph found in the room under the hardware store." Then, just like a group of school children waiting for the ice cream man to stop so they could get their treat, everyone went and crowded around the wagon to see what was in the box. Arthur jumped down from the wagon and pointed to the metal box.

"That thing weights as much as four toilets," he said. "There must be something really valuable inside."

I took the brass key out of my pocket and handed it to Ralph. "It's all yours," I said.

Ralph looked at his father. "Go ahead, son, you deserve it," he said, nodding his head. Ralph put the key into the lock and turned until it clicked open. He removed the lock and slowly lifted the hasp. He took a deep breath then opened the box. Bright gold coins tumbled out and rolled across the wagon bed. Ralph reached into the box and grabbed a handful of coins. Underneath the coins, at the bottom of the box, were four solid gold bars. A smile swept across Ralph's face.

"See, Pop, what did I tell you!" he said, almost shouting. Ralph's father grabbed him and gently hugged him.

"You did well, son," he said. "I'm proud of you."

While Ralph celebrated with his family, Becky came up behind me and punched me in the arm.

"Hey…what was that for?" I asked.

"Because I'm not supposed to do this!" she said, grabbing me and kissing me on the cheek. With her arms still around my neck, she whispered in my ear, "Good job, Country Boy… good job."

THE END